SIL

STI

OVER 100
GREAT NOVELS
OF
EROTIC DOMINATION

If you like one you will probably like the rest

NEW TITLES EVERY MONTH

All titles in print are now available from:

www.adultbookshops.com

If you want to be on our confidential mailing list for our Readers' Club
Magazine (with extracts from past and forthcoming titles) write to:

SILVER MOON READER SERVICES

Shadowline Publishing Ltd
No 2 Granary House
Ropery Road
Gainsborough
DN21 2NS
United Kingdom

telephone: 01427 611697
Fax: 01427 611776

NEW AUTHORS WELCOME

Please send submissions to
Silver Moon Books Ltd.
PO Box 5663
Nottingham
NG3 6PJ
or
editor@babash.com

First published 2006 Silver Moon Books
ISBN 1-903687-80-2
© 2006,7 Josephine Scott

A SLAVE IN TIME

BY

JOSEPHINE SCOTT

Originally published as 'The Time of her Life' by Nexus

ALSO BY JOSEPHINE SCOTT
WHEN THE MASTER SPEAKS

CHAPTER 1: THEN

Laughter and talk, stiff skirts sweeping the rush-covered floor, jewels sparkling in the light from the fire and the flaming sconces set high on walls. Light also glanced from lace collars; fans fluttered and created their own flares of colour. Small pointed beards, small moustaches, long flowing hair; so elegant these men, so naturally graceful in ribbons and silks. So unlike the men Abigail was used to.

An air of expectation hung over everything, keen glances turning toward the far door where someone was going to make an entrance.

Abigail moved carefully along the stone wall, her naked thighs whispering under her skirts, quim aching with desire - would this be the night she would find the nerve to approach him? She caught sight of herself in a polished shield, glad to see her black hair was dressed just as the ladies had done theirs, with combs and curls, and that the floury mask she had applied fitted well with the look most ladies wore. The shield distorted the shape of her face; she knew it was oval, but in the reflection it was more elongated. People looked because she was a stranger, not because she looked out of place.

She hoped her lace collar didn't appear too machine-made. It was different from the rich, expensive and beautiful lace they wore. Abigail couldn't afford hand-made lace.

She moved on toward a tall, clouded window, apologising with a nod and a smile for disturbing guests. She received more curious looks but people soon turned away again, back to the door.

Waiting.

A fanfare of trumpets shook castle walls, a boy herald in scarlet doublet and leggings, angelic face, dark hair, perhaps ten years old, stepped in front of the fire, and everyone fell silent.

"My Lord Danverson bids you welcome to the Midsummer Ball!" The high-pitched childish voice carried to the minstrels' gallery. On cue, Lord Danverson entered the hall, ermine robe careless around his shoulders, a doublet glistening with jewels sparkling from the rushlights, huge leather boots rustling as he walked. Abigail noted (again) the broad shoulders, strong legs and harsh profile. She also noticed that no woman accompanied him (again).

"Welcome!" His voice filled corners where shadows hung and ghosts lingered. Someone - a trusted man servant? - handed him a tankard of ale, the wood polished and shining like pewter. "Welcome to Castle Danverson. Musicians, play!" A huge roar went up as he waved the tankard high in the air, foam and ale spilling on to dogs which scampered, barking, at his feet, affected by the tangible excitement of the crowd.

Music began to fill the air, competing with voices and roaring laughter.

"And, people, eat!" Another roar, larger and louder than the first, shook dust from the rafters. Abigail brushed smuts from her scarlet dress, smoothed the black overskirt, tugged at the starched collar and pushed the choker into place. She had an appearance to maintain in the eyes of strangers.

Men fell on the food with hearty appetites. Women hung back, waiting for the men to clear a space for them. Food. It was the one thing she couldn't do. Not here. She turned back to the window, looked out at rolling downland, fields cultivated in small strips of regular appearance and size. Over it all hung the indefinable sadness of twilight, sun giving way to dark, pinkness giving way to the pressure of purple and then black.

Abigail wished the window was open so she could smell the sadness that tinged the land. It stirred her each time she came here.

"I do not remember seeing you before." A wave of perfume washed around her as Abigail turned to see a dark-haired woman smiling, eyes bright with curiosity. She was wearing a dress of blue overlaying a rich petticoat of gold silk; she had a fluttering fan and eyelashes and a coy smile. Abigail wished she had a chance to get her hands on a dress like that. Or a smile like that.

"No, I ... come from ... far away, just for the ball." Weak, even to her ears. "My Lord's reputation has spread some distance away." That was safe, surely.

"Did you see my Lord's prowess with the falcon in the hunt today?"

"I would rather see my Lord's prowess in bed at night!"

Abigail took a chance with boldness, trusting the look in the eyes didn't let her down. They were talking of the same thing, surely.

The woman's laugh was short and harsh.

"Not I! They say he is a cruel man with a taste for hurting women. But I admire a man who hunts and who can control the falcon as well as my Lord does."

"I would take my chances if I could bed him, for all that."

Abigail glanced at her companion, hoping she'd said it right. There seemed no hint of confusion or suspicion. Talking under rather than over the sound of the minstrels in the gallery helped cover some of the defects in her accent.

"Dance!" bellowed Lord Danverson. Abigail's companion smiled, accepted the arm of a tall blond man in a large padded green doublet encrusted with gold, and moved gracefully into the dance.

"You must talk with me again," she murmured as she left.

Abigail leaned against the windowsill and watched. The castle hall was alive with swirling skirts, lace and gold trimmings. Ladies with starched collars framing their faces rested ring-encrusted hands on their partners' arms, creating a kaleidoscope of colour and movement. Sword hilts sparkled with jewels as the owners moved, hands rarely far from their sides, always alert for any sign of trouble. Were men never at ease with themselves, Abigail wondered?

Smoke from the huge fires hung over everything, disturbed by dancers, by sudden loud shouts from groups of men exchanging pleasantries and jokes at others' expense, standing in corners and near the table.

Abigail shivered. Midsummer, yet it was cold; the fires were welcome. Some guests hugged the flames, in danger of scorching by sparks which leapt from logs. Steam rose from food set out along vast tables stood four square to the floor. Rushes were kicked aside as dancers moved apart and together, swung apart and together again in intricate courtship. Over it all hung the mingled scent of wood ash, food, perfume, dust, mould and body odour. Yet it didn't seem unpleasant to her.

Lord Danverson seemed to be everywhere at once, drinking, shouting, dancing with abandon and gusto, a man who lived life to the full. Abigail saw him look at her, saw the appreciative smile, knew scarlet silk suited her well and that her face was the equal of any at the Midsummer Ball that night.

The dance ended. Lord Danverson left his partner and pushed his way past the guests to approach her.

"Might I enquire if you are enjoying the ball?"

"Yes, my Lord."

"I have seen you here before, but I do not know your name or where you have your home."

"My Lord, I have been a guest at your celebrations on other occasions. I live in a village not far from here. You may know it: Walchurch."

"I know it, but I have no knowledge of the families who live there. And your name?"

A great roar of laughter went up behind Lord Danverson. He smiled and edged closer to Abigail, pinning her against cold stone. Musicians began another dance. Someone bumped into Abigail, half apologised as they moved away, spilling ale from a pewter tankard.

"Abigail Brandon, my Lord." She curtsied as elegantly as she could.

"And on whose arm did you come to the ball tonight?" he leaned against the sill, close, almost whispering. Abigail strained to catch the words.

"I came alone, to see my Lord Danverson."

"Wait for me in my room." It was an order, not a request.

"Yes, my Lord." No questions asked. Accepted. Just as she hoped. He walked away, a smile twisting his dark face. Abigail saw a pageboy standing to one side, anxious, ready to move at command. She beckoned to him.

"Madam?"

"Which is my Lord Danverson's room?"

"On the floor above the gallery, four doors along, a room with blue tapestries and a large bed."

"Thank you. Not a word now, why or what I asked."

The pageboy nodded. He had seen his Lord with her and knew not to ask any questions.

Abigail slipped quietly away, ducking invitations to dance with a smile and shake of her head. Her companion in blue and gold half raised a hand, saw Abigail was leaving and turned back to her companion. Relief - for had she seen machine stitching on the dress, she might have asked questions Abigail could not answer. Not here, not now.

She hurried up the stairs, slippers clicking on the worn stone and thighs whispering their secret as moisture began to seep onto the skin, adding to her barely contained excitement. He had noticed her, he wanted her, he had spoken to her and ordered her to his room. This night she could have him for her very own.

The gallery was chill, the sun leaving the sky to creeping hands of darkness. Thick stone walls had hardly time to become warm before night caught them in an icy grip. Feeble rush lamps flickered and flared in draughts which found their way through velvet hangings and tapestries. She thought (again) England in the summer of 1625 was not really warm enough for her liking.

Lord Danverson's room. The bed was indeed large, draped with blue hangings of rich velvet. It held his scent, smoke, ale, tobacco, leather and cotton. Clothes tossed to one side held the smell of the hunt: horses and woods, blood and sweat. A huge chest stood against a wall, carved with a hunting scene. Abigail ran her hands over it, appreciating the workmanship. Back home, such things were only found in museums, or expensive antique shops. The thought occurred to her that she could become an eminent historian with first-hand knowledge of furniture and antiques, but then they'd wonder how she knew.

And there was the mirror in its ornate frame, hanging over the mantelpiece. It had been moved. Last time it was in one of the drawing rooms, framed by tapestries with wild hunting scenes and mythological stories on them. It had been easy to find. This was pure luck.

She was grateful for the small fire. Crouching down and lifting her heavy petticoats, she daydreamed. He was as handsome as before, strong long jaw, short pointed beard in the fashion of the day. Dark piercing eyes, Roman nose, a strong handsome face. Would he be good, this man of the manor, of the land, of the whole damn county, by the look of him? Would he be hard and long and would he satisfy her? She could but hope. Surely she hadn't made the journey back again for nothing!

And he had remembered her! Abigail's brief appearances at the castle on the earlier Midwinter and Midsummer feasts had been cautious, moving carefully through the guests, not catching anyone's eye, but waiting her chance. This time she decided to be bold, to experience the man for her own self.

He was long in coming. She huddled on a small stool, then sat on the floor, and finally lay down on a large fur rug stretched before the hearth, dozing and starting awake a dozen times before the door scraped open and she heard slippers coming in.

"I thought you might have left with the others." Slurred with drink, but firm enough for all that. Close to, he was as exciting as she had thought earlier, a lust gleaming in his eyes that brought his face alight. Abigail stood and stretched her arms around his neck, pulling him close, feeling dark stubble graze her face. She breathed in musk, the smell of food, sweat, smoke and manliness that was the greatest aphrodisiac of all. If only it could be bottled and sold! His arms went round her, iron bands holding her close. He darted kisses at her throat, her temple, her nose. She leaned back to look at him.

"My Lord said to wait."

"Yes, but the ball went on longer than I thought."

"I would have waited a thousand days for my Lord," she whispered, pressing against him his muscles hard through her layers of petticoats and hoops. The swelling was there. Her body rarely betrayed her - it conquered the men every time. That and her boldness; they could never stand up to that.

Between kisses he protested: "I do not know who you are..."

"But you do. Abigail Brandon, of Walchurch. What more could my Lord ask? Come." She led him to the bed, pulling on one work-hardened hand, and sat him on the edge of the huge goose-feather mattress. Then she disrobed slowly, watching his eyes, knowing his excitement. Her soft white skin, heavy full breasts with large nipples, and her plucked pussy, something surely no 17th century man had ever seen, were good for all men. His eyes grew wide and a hand reached out to touch her quim, sliding over the silky whiteness, amazed.

"I have never seen such things - not in my furthest journeyings."

"It is for you and you alone," she whispered, drawing closer to him. He reached out again, hands sliding over her full hips, touching her breasts, the nipples coming erect at his touch. She drew in her breath sharply as one hand found her spine, a finger tracing the length, cupping and smoothing and turning to admire her shape from all angles.

Then he stood up, held her close, kissed her deeply, his breath smelling and tasting of ale and strong meat, a smoky musky smell and taste that thrilled almost as much as the look of his hard muscular body. She moved cautiously against him, not wanting to hurry but wanting him to please, please fuck her and soon. Wet now, wet and willing.

Lord Danverson moved suddenly, pushing her down onto the bed and parting her legs, staring at her as he swiftly undressed, tossing his clothes onto another wild heap on the floor. Then he stood erect, strong, gleaming with lust. She held out her arms, almost groaning at the sight of him. She had waited, she had schemed to get back here, and it had been worth every moment for the sight of him alone.

He climbed onto the bed, knelt between her legs, touched with both hands, letting his fingers slide down her thighs, back up around her hips, up to her navel, under her shaved armpits. He raised his eyebrows but said nothing. She stared at him, tongue pressing between her teeth, sometimes licking her lips, finding him for herself, the heavy balls, hairy and firm, the thick handful she held, touched, caressed, then reached for his buttocks as best she could, grabbing his muscled things, catching his hands at times and pressing them to her quim, begging him without words to do it now.

The length and thickness of his member surprised, shocked, thrilled her as it slid home into her warm waiting body. It filled her completely, pressed against every nerve ending she had. He thrust hard, grunting with pleasure, holding both cheeks in his large hands, again and again finding every part of her. She cried out in sheer pleasure, clawing nails down his back. Every atom reacted to the feeling, shaking her to her toes, she all but swooned. He thrust harder and yet harder, pushing her into the mattress of feather and down. She cried out again, climaxing twice in a blinding sweep of feeling which shut out all thought, all consideration and then swept over her again as he finally came shuddering into her.

He raised himself up and looked at Abigail, an unreadable look, stern yet wondering. She tried to bring herself back down from the high. Something was going on here, she had to cope with it, yet she was longing for more.

Try persuasion.

"Did I please my Lord?" Oh do it again, she thought desperately, do it again! Instead he got up, snatched a robe, flung it around his shoulders and paced the floor. He stopped at times to stare at Abigail, his face unreadable in the mix of light from the rapidly diminishing candle he had brought to his room, and the slowly dying fire.

"You pleased me, but there is something wrong, something I dislike."

"My Lord?"

He appeared to come to a decision and turned toward the bedroom door. "It is the boldness, I think. I can deal with that and I will. Page!"

The door sprang open as if by magic and a small boy stood there, blinking sleep from his eyes.

"Sire?"

"Fetch me a birch!"

The boy looked scared but said "Sire!" and the door closed again.

"A ... birch?" stammered Abigail, pushing herself up the bed, getting away from the gleam of pure malice which had replaced the one of lust.

"A birch, my lady, a birch - for the pretty cheeks which were so keen to be dealt with in one way must be dealt with in another." He leaned across the bed and caught hold of her wrists with hands as hard as iron, dragging her toward the bedpost. Then she was on her feet, both hands being held together on one side of the post, shivering with post orgasmic pleasure and a touch of fear. Events were taking a turn she had not anticipated and it was a bit scary. Lord Danverson grinned as he

14

slid the girdle from his robe and bound her wrists tightly with the silken length. Around and around her wrists, pulling her veins close together, so close she could feel her pulse. Abigail bit her lips, looked at Lord Danverson with pleading eyes, saying 'let me go' without uttering the words.

Suddenly she remembered the woman from the ball:

'Not I, for they say he is a cruel man with a taste for hurting women.'

"I do not know from where you came, or why you are here with me, but those who offer their bodies are wanton hussies and are dealt with in the time-honoured way, madam." The last word was said with sarcasm and malice. The gleam of lust was back again - this man did indeed have a taste for hurting women. Abigail was suddenly very cold. His come trickled down her thigh, cool and sticky and she became aware of a real tinge of fear for the first time since she had started visiting Castle Danverson.

But underneath the fear was the excitement of yet another new experience and she knew that, even if she could see herself in the mirror, she wouldn't. Wouldn't send herself dizzyingly flying forward through hundreds of years. To safety.

Your choice. You vowed to take whatever was given to you in this time, no matter what.

But a birch? Fear sat coppery-tasting in her mouth, her body shivering despite the fire. She could not see Lord Danverson but she sensed him standing very still, very tense, very exited, and wondered again what was to happen. One thing was sure: she could not twist this man around her finger as she had the others, oh so many others.

It seemed an age before the door opened again and the small boy's voice said: "The birch, sire."

The door closed. Lord Danverson had not spoken. Abigail stared at the rich hangings of the four poster bed, stared at the carved headboard with its cornucopia of fruit and birds, felt rather than saw him walk around her, eyeing her carefully.

"Now, madam, we will deal with wanton hussies who offer themselves to their Lord." A thousand bees stung her at once as the birch connected with her bare bottom. She cried out, gasping in pain and shock as it landed, again and again.

"On my territory, women are taught to obey their men in all things and that, madam, includes the question of who he is to take to his bed." The many strands found her, tiny buds causing their own pain, sharp wet twigs flexible enough to bend on impact, to send fire through her. Abigail had never known such a thing: no one had ever hurt her before. She fought the pain and the bonds, but he went on birching her, forcing her into the post, her pubis grinding against the carving as she tried to squirm away from the stinging, biting, burning sensation. Tears coursed down her face, tears of helplessness as much as in cursing herself for her stupidity. Never get out of sight of the mirror! she told herself, crying out as the birch found her again.

"My sentence is always the same for those who commit misdemeanours here, madam." A pause in the agony, just his relentless voice lecturing her on the wilful nature of her crime. Lord Danverson was not a man to be crossed at any time!

Oh let that be it! she pleaded and prayed silently, waiting, quivering, hurting, as he walked backwards and forwards, slippers hushing on the wooden floor. Somehow she knew it would be a waste of breath to plead aloud for mercy and clemency.

"My sentences for wayward hussies, women who

should know better, is 50 strokes of the birch. Madam, you have had 25. There are 25 to go."

She was hurting so much, surely he had drawn blood! No one could hurt this much and not bleed!

"Stand and wait."

She had no choice, hands bound round the post as they were. Tears continued to pour down her face, she longed to wipe them away.

"Sire..."

"Be silent! It is not done for a woman to entice a man in such a way - no respectable woman! You came with no man, I asked them all! You belong to no one! Did you come with the intention of finding my room? Be warned, wench, I do not usually consort with wanton women but it is midsummer and you intrigued me. Now you will pay the price of that intrigue, whoever you are."

Abigail bit her lips, afraid of spilling the truth. Not that Lord Danverson would believe she had come from hundreds of years in the future, anyway.

He began to birch her again, this time finding her thighs and legs. The pain was intense and gave her superhuman strength. Even as she cried out her despair and fear, the girdle gave way and she was free. She looked at Lord Danverson, registered his surprise, shock and outrage, cast one despairing glance into the mirror and was...

CHAPTER TWO: NOW

The mirror glared at her, defying her to look into it, to see the reddened eyes and streaked face she could feel. Before then -

No, not you, mirror! The other one, the safe one.

Abby looked at herself in the full length mirror, saw the vivid red marks, wondered why she wasn't bleeding. How could she be so hurt and not bleed?

I shouldn't have let him get that close, or get myself that far from the mirror! I shouldn't have let him bind me. I should not have... she raved at herself silently.

But I did. And now I'm suffering. Oh it hurts! Can't sit, lie or stand properly - fool, Abby, fool!

She hurried into the bathroom and stood under the shower, washing away odours, some of the soreness, and Lord Danverson's come. As she showered, she thought.

His come. I have a problem. This is my problem. All philosophers and scientists and those who should know about such things say if we travel back in time and disrupt in the slightest way any particle of that time, if we consume food, water, even air, we disturb future generations. Food that we have taken should and could have been given to another. If that person died for lack of it, then a whole generation may not appear, which would alter the future.

On the other hand, what if I was intended to go and take that food, that air, that come... will anyone ever really know?

Let's face this fact. I carry a man's sperm within me. I carry what could be his heirs. Yet the world I come back to... Is the same.

As far as I know.

Out there, perhaps, is a strange gap in a family tree, a

line that never happened, a dynasty which did not occur. A brilliant invention that was never created. Who can say? I have no way of knowing. I only know this. I come back to a world I know is identical to the one I left.

I come back at the moment I left it, even though I might be gone for hours. I come back - Satisfied.

Chapter 3 Now

Abby pushed open the door to the offices of Brooks, Wilkins & Co., and walked in, greeted by the familiar smell of old dust, mouldering papers, pink tape and polish.

"Morning, Abby, nice weekend?" The bright, bubbly young girl behind the reception desk smiled through shocking-pink lipstick.

"Hi, Jane. Not bad, how about you?"

"Oh good, good. Ronnie took me to see that film at the Odeon. You know, the new Dracula one."

Abby paused, resting her shoulder bag on the reception desk, pushing a few slit envelopes out of the way.

"Is it any good?"

"Sure is. There's this scene - " The switchboard buzzed angrily. "Oh damn! Starting early this morning." She turned away. "Tell you later. Good morning, Brooks Wilkins & Co., Can I help you?"

Abby hurried up the stairs to her small office, waving to the other secretaries as she passed their room.

"Hi Abby! Hey, you look tired, heavy weekend?"

"Sure was, Sue. Catch you later."

Abby dropped her bag behind her desk and went to struggle with the old sash window. It always stuck; it did again today. What happened to the theory that wood swelled in damp weather and dried out in the hot weather? This window stuck, no matter what was outside: rain, hail or sun.

It was stiflingly hot in the small room. The spider plant on top of the filing cabinet nodded sagely as the summer breeze came in the now opened window, stirring the hot air. Abby sank down in her chair and took a mirror out of the personal drawer. She was tired. Today her black hair had lost some of its lustre, dulled by dust and heat perhaps, despite a good shampoo in the morning, and her blue eyes were encircled with dark rings. She put the mirror away, switched on her word processor and looked at the desk. Mr. Wilkins had been busy, a tape was waiting for her on top of a pile of files. Better get going I suppose, she thought.

Before she could put her earphones in, the telephone rang, making her jump. God, nerves are bad.

"Abby, Kenneth Thompson on the line."

"Right."

"Hi, Abby, busy?"

"Hello, Kenneth, yes, busy as always. How can I help?"

"Well, this is a lunch invite. How about going out to the Patson Motel for lunch, pick you up about 1.30?"

"Fine."

"Good. See you later."

Abby replaced the phone and looked at the screen. Damn, if she had entertained any idea there was a lunch date in the offing she wouldn't have travelled last night! Now look, honour bound to go out - "keep the clients happy, Abigail" she could almost hear Mr. Wilkins saying before she got to his room to tell him. Lunch, and she had to sit still, despite her lines and soreness!

A balding head wearing glasses peered round the door.

"Morning, Abigail."

"Morning, Mr. Wilkins. Kenneth Thompson just phoned to invite me to lunch. I was about to come and tell you. Is that all right?"

"Of course. Keep the clients happy, Abigail. See if you can secure some financial work from him on top of the boring old accident stuff."

"I'll try."

"I have to be in court in half an hour. Take all calls for me, will you?"

"Of course, Mr. Wilkins."

That accounted for the early pile of work. Mr. Wilkins was too conscientious to go off to court for a morning without leaving his secretary a considerable amount of typing. Abby sighed and picked up the earphones again.

She was deep in some complicated Instructions to Counsel when Jane put her head round the door, startling her. God, my nerves, she thought, angry with herself. Must be jangling from yesterday!

"Abby, there's a client downstairs, wants to see Mr. Wilkins urgent, and I don't know what he's done with his diary."

"Okay, Jane, I'll see to it."

Abby pushed back her chair, glad of the chance to stand up for a while, and went into Mr. Wilkins' dusty crowded office, avoiding the black japanned gold-letter boxes (death to many pairs of tights in the past) and searched the desk for the diary, unearthing it from beneath a pile of photographs of a crash, corpse still in place. She averted her gaze and wondered why. They were only monochrome images after all.

Much as I viewed the past, until I got the mirror, she thought, going down the stairs. Now I know it's -

In reception, Abby stopped dead as if struck by lightning.

The woman, who was in the act of rising from the padded bench, also stopped. Recognition flew between them. The woman was dark-haired, and wearing a blue suit with a gold blouse. Her eyes were flashing curiosity.

"I don't remember seeing you before." Abrupt, almost curt.

"I... I've not long moved here. I'm Mr. Wilkin's secretary."

'I do not remember seeing you before.'

'No, I... come from ... far away just for the ball. My

Lord's reputation has spread some distance away.'

'Did you see my Lord's prowess with the falcon in the hunt today?'

'I would rather see my Lord's prowess in bed at night!'

And she had and it had been - an experience.

"I'm sure I've seen you somewhere before." The woman frowned. Abby almost spoke and then bit her tongue, hard.

"Mr. Wilkins is in court this morning but he has some time free this afternoon, three-thirty. Would you like to come and see him then?"

"Yes, that should be all right."

"Your name is - ?"

"Mrs. Dawson-Page. I ... want to see him about a financial settlement. I'm separating from my husband."

And is your husband a tall blond man who moves with the grace of a jungle cat? But the question stayed unasked and unanswered.

A further thought jumped into Abby's head as she wrote in the diary.

Is Mrs. Dawson-Page going off with a tall blond man who moves with the grace of a jungle cat?

Still looking puzzled, Mrs. Dawson-Page left the reception area. Jane turned to Abby.

"Odd woman. Seemed as though something hit her like a thunderbolt when you came down the stairs, Abby."

"She seems to think she's seen me before, and I haven't seen her."

Oh but I have.

"Coffee won't be long. Let me get this copying done for Mr. Brooks."

"Fine. By the way, I'm going to lunch with Kenneth Thompson at one-thirty."

"Lucky you!"

23

Lucky me, thought Abby, going back to her office. Lucky me with no man around, just some admirers who are pests at the best of times and sex maniacs at the worst, but let's face it .. useless sex maniacs. If they were any good I'd not have to rely on taking myself in hand or using a plastic dildo...

Lunch, tinkle of silvery cutlery scraping plates, muted sound of plates scraping fine white linen, rustle of unrolling napkins, gentle trickling of fine wine being poured into glasses which rang at the touch of a nail, tempting aroma of finely cooked food - not like the spit-roasted and boiled-to-death food on the table at the Danverson's midsummer ball! What would happen if I ate anything when I was there? Or drank water, or took anything other than come?

"You're shifting around on that seat as if you've been spanked!" Kenneth Thompson looked through fine-rimmed glasses and smiled, half puzzled, half knowing. Abby blushed.

"Sorry, just thinking."

"Tell me: you've been very quiet this time, not your usual bubbly self."

"This is going to sound silly - " she broke off, cutting pale pink roast beef which slid apart under her knife.

"It's you, me and the waiter and he isn't listening."

The other diners were busy with their meals. Alongside them the huge plate-glass window showed the busy road, flushed with cars of all shades, noisy with trucks bearing huge painted slogans that shouted commerce to the world. The soundless waiters moved as if on castors, distributing wine, food and calorie-uncontrolled desserts.

"I started a book last night, just some thoughts, and it's rather taken over."

As good a story as any, and it's half true. I may well write it all down one day!

"A book! Sounds interesting. Tell me," and the face went into the 'I'm interested' pose that she knew so well. Insurance Brokers looked the same, no matter what you were talking about. They just needed to give the impression of listening.

"I have this idea - of a heroine who finds a mirror in an old shop, not an antique shop, you understand, but one of those house clearance places. There's this mirror on the wall, ornate gilt frame, very expensive and old-looking, but the thing is ... it isn't showing what it's facing. There's no reflection."

"A supernatural book."

"More sci-fi, I think. You see, when my heroine looks into the mirror, she flies back to some point in the past. She controls how and where she goes by wearing the appropriate costume. For example, if she's wearing an Edwardian outfit, that's where she goes."

"And has adventures. Sound good." The 'I'm interested' look became real for the first time. "How would she get hold of the costumes?"

"She does a bit of part-time acting with the local amateur dramatics society."

"Yes, of course. As you do."

Yes, I do, and I'll be there tonight at the King's Theatre, raiding the costume department. I want another adventure. The more I have, the more I want!

She frowned suddenly. Shifting around as if I've been spanked. Does he know what it would be like, to see a woman sitting before him who had been spanked?

She cleared the frown before it could take hold.

There was time enough to consider that thought, later.

"How much have you done of this book?" The wine was going down fast. He'd had a bit too much and a flush had suffused his face, heading for the pale green Rael Brook collar that sat above his silk tie.

"I sketched out some plot lines last night and wrote the opening pages."

"Got a title, has it?"

Come on, Abby, think!

"A Slave in Time."

"And are you going to write it? I mean, this isn't just an idea that'll go nowhere, is it?"

"I'm going to write it."

"Good." The smile was real, the interest genuine. That much she did understand. "What are you doing at the theatre at the moment?"

"A drama set in the time of Charles I, court and officials and mistresses, all sorts of intrigue."

"That's your starting point for the book, then, the time of Charles I, whenever that was."

"1625," she said.

He raised his eyebrows. "You've done your research." He beckoned to the waiter. "Let me know how it goes. I'm interested, really I am."

Not as much as I am.

The bill was settled with a flash of plastic. (What would Lord Danverson think of that; and come to think of it, what was Lord Danverson's name? Bedded by someone whose name she didn't know!)

The journey back to the office was conducted in high spirits and a promise of more financial work. Mr. Wilkins'll be pleased, thought Abby, going back to her desk, pretending not to see Jane's envious look and Sue's wink as she passed.

"It's called keeping the clients happy" she told herself, as the pile of files continued to glare at her. At least they hadn't been added to while she was out, although the pile of telephone messages had. Sighing, she pulled the phone over and began to call the clients.

More clients to keep happy.

What about me?

I like the book idea. I'm going to write it. As soon as I get home I'll do what I told Kenneth I'd already done, and perhaps ...

Make some money as well as having adventures.

Why can't I write about what I experience?

Wow! What a thought! Truth on paper and no one but no one would know it was real!

"Hello, Johnson Bailey? This is Mr. Wilkins's secretary at Brooks Wilkins & Co." ...

"Listen, people, we have a problem." Alfred Fitzpaine, accountant by day, stage manager at night. Abby smiled to herself. How strange it was that when people got into a theatre, they threw off inhibitions and became totally different. She knew Alfred very well from work, and knew he was normally a quiet man whose voice barely rose above a whisper. But here, in the echoing auditorium of the King's Theatre/Community Centre, he boomed and directed, ordered and at times even stormed about. Will the real Alfred Fitzpaine please step forward?

He started on about set designs, props needed urgently to complete the scenario and Abby let her mind wander.

"... and then there's the question of costume. I want each of you to take your costume away with you and get it fitted properly, make sure you feel at home in it, walk around in it. You can't be at home in it until everything comes naturally, climbing steps, sitting, standing, moving, without catching everything on the tables! Particularly you men, you're not used to having a heavy sword hanging by your side and it's a tall order for you to move around the stage."

The realisation struck Abby like the thunderbolt she was sure had struck Mrs Dawson-Page that afternoon.

The red-and-black dress. It was still in Lord Danverson's room along with a heap of petticoats and a chemise, stockings and even her slippers! All there, all -

Machine-stitched and made of materials not found in that time.

Damn and blast and damn again! I have to get back there; I have to rescue the clothes!

"Abby, I've decided I'd rather you wore a more

sombre dress than originally planned. I think the red and black is too startling for a goodwife, so would you mind wearing a purple?"

"Of course not."

"You can bring the red and black one back next rehearsal. Stevie darling, if Abby brings the red and black one, would you like it? I think with your blonde hat it will look quite striking."

First I have to get it.

Rehearsals seemed to last forever. Stevie was in one of her petulant moods and refused to speak above a normal voice, no matter that Alfred was sitting halfway back from the stage and couldn't hear a thing. Abby felt oddly out of place in jeans and shirt. She knew Alfred was right, you needed to wear the costumes to get it right. After all, she had put on a superb performance for Castle Danverson and its guests yesterday.

Yesterday? Was that all it was? It felt like months ago! The red lines had faded, leaving just a few marks here and there for the mirror to show her that morning, leaving just the sense of loss and a touch of melancholy.

At last the rehearsal was called to a halt, Stevie pouted off the stage, Abby swept up the purple dress, stroked the thick lace collar and huge sleeves and smiled.

Now she had something to go back in.

Chapter 5: Then

The castle stood dreaming under the crescent-shaped midsummer moon, which was lying on its back in the blue-purple sky. Somewhere an owl hooted, a fox barked and the dogs murmured in their sleep, scratching at the fur rug and chasing rabbits in their dreams.

Abigail slipped softly through the hall, barefoot, tip-toeing over ice-cold stones and rustling rushes. The lingering scent of ale and food seemed to hold the sound of voices and music, the castle itself hung over from the midsummer ball. A good time was had by all.

A brindle bitch raised her head and growled deep in her throat. Abigail held out her hand. The dog reluctantly got to her feet, came over and sniffed the outstretched hand, taking the offer of friendship for what it was - a mere interruption to dreams. It went back to the warmth of the glowing embers.

Stone stairs did not creak, and Abigail slid quietly along against the banister, holding on to the thick oak rail with one hand to guide her. Torchlight flickered and went out; only the crescent moon, thin and unwilling, shone onto the landing. Four doors along.

The pageboy sleeping at the door opened his eyes wide in shock and almost shrieked. Abigail put one hand to her lips and held the other out to touch him, but he fled in sheer terror.

The latch clicked loud enough to rouse the dead of Walchurch, but Lord Danverson slept on.

And there, piled neatly on the chest, lay her dress, petticoats, chemise and slippers. Abigail put the slippers on and hung the clothes over her arm. Lord Danverson twisted and turned on the bed but showed no signs of waking. It was possible the ale would keep him sleeping for some time. In the morning, no doubt with a sore head and bad temper, perhaps he would not remember the clothes.

She could but hope.

One glance in the ornate mirror and she was...

CHAPTER 6: NOW

Back in her room.

The mirror reflected ancient light from long-gone torches, the white nightmare look of the pageboy's terror, the crescent moon and all the silvered countryside beyond the smoky windows.

The temptation to stand in front of the mirror again was overwhelming, but Abby turned away, touched with a melancholy she could not define. She undressed and dropped the purple gown on the couch, determined not to travel again tonight but bothered by her longing to go back immediately to that time.

She hung the red dress behind the door, safely way from the mirror's grasp. Tomorrow would be time enough to return it to the King's Theatre wardrobe department, and tomorrow would be soon enough to plan another adventure.

Where to this time?

CHAPTER 7: THEN

The gathering was High Society, honourables and ladies, frilled silk and feather outfits, the men straining against waistcoats controlled by large gold chains which encircled them. The talk was of money and Society even more elvated than that gathered in the elegant drawing room.

Abigail moved slowly around the perimeters of the crowd, seeking out a worthwhile prey. Women smiled over fans or dainty handkerchiefs, men eyed her openly. She knew the lilac silk suited to perfection, her dark hair curled elegantly in all the right places and her lips pouted enough to attract attention. But then, any woman alone would attract attention.

"Haven't I seen you before?" The lady's look travelled over the outfit, from buttoned boots to kid gloves, the parasol hinged and ruffled hanging nonchalantly at her side. Abigail smiled and nodded, said nothing, moved on. The woman turned back to her friends, chattering earnestly behind a gloved hand ringed with heavy jewels.

"And the Prince of Wales said - " The man broke off and peered at Abigail through a monocle attached to his body by black silk. "By Jove, madam, you're a fine sight to behold!"

"Why thank you, kind sir." Abigail did a mock curtsey and edged past, heading through clouds of delicate perfume and richness of sherry in Waterford crystal, making for the tall, distinguished white-haired man she saw standing alone by the bay window. He looked oddly sad - convention dictated that you should wear a smile even if you were dying, inside or out.

"A fine gathering." He spoke looking out of the window, not looking in her direction.

"I thought so."

He turned suddenly, took in her alluring look and had the grace to blush.

"My apologies, madam, I thought you were our hostess."

"I think she is somewhere..." Abigail gestured toward a large group, hoping against hope that the hostess, whoever that might be, was prominently on display.

The man nodded, the silver-white hair hardy moving. Abigail took in the expensive cut of the suit, diamond stick-pin in the tie, thickness of the gold chain, and gambled. "'You are here alone, sir?"

"I am, for my wife is at home suffering from some ague or other."

"I am right sorry to hear that."

He took her hand, looked into her eyes. "Something about you tells me ..."

"What?"

"Nothing." He shook his head. "Are you alone, madam?"

"I am." No explanation. Abigail hoped he wouldn't ask for one.

"I admire your dress."

"Thank you. I admire your suit." She looked around, seemingly impatient with the party while he laughed with genuine humour. "Is there somewhere we can... talk?"

"We could go to my club."

"A wonderful idea." Abigail accepted the proffered arm, walked past scandalised ladies who stood with mouths and eyes agape at her effrontery. Men smirked and hid their thoughts behind their hands. One of the ladies bustled over, a migraine vision of screaming cerise silk and outrageous makeup.

"Sir Anthony, you're not leaving us already?" Abigail

was blatantly ignored.

"This lady feels a little faint, my dear Myrtle. I am taking her for a little air. And then perhaps I should be going, for you know my dear lady wife is not at all well at the moment."

"Certainly, of course, I understand." Her look swept Abigail from head to foot, while the curl of the lip said volumes. But she was also bursting with curiosity. Surely she hadn't been invited - no one knew who she was - what was she doing here, in this gathering of London's most famous?

"Please do give Lady Caroline my sincere condolences on her poor state of health and tell her I hope to see her at bridge next Tuesday." Gushing with insincerity. A silence had fallen over the party, a silence profound enough to be cut with a silver cake knife. Abigail stifled a giggle, turned it into a small cough. She put on a severe face, hoping she looked paler than she felt.

"Thank you, I must go. Coming, my dear?" Sir Anthony had reacted to the slight pressure she put on his arm with consummate skill.

The bubble of voices - "Who is that woman, how did she get here, who brought her? My dear, you must tell all!" almost trapped them before the door closed on the train of Abigail's dress. She tugged at it and felt it tear. What the hell, it didn't matter, it was just a costume.

The street was busy with hansom cabs and boys running messages, peddlars with their wares on trays, bells and loud voices assaulting her on all sides.

"Violets, violets for the lady?" The tattered clothes could scarcely have kept the old woman warm. Sir Anthony tossed a few coins into the basket and chose the choicest flowers for Abigail. She accepted them with a smile and tucked them into her neckline, noting how well they went with the lilac silk.

"I can understand Myrtle's confusion, for you are not one of her usual guests." A small dog ran past, yapping madly. A ragged boy chased after it, screaming and waving a stick. Abigail smiled and looked up into the man's deep blue eyes.

"I am not one of Myrtle's guests. I just... appeared there."

"Of course you did, like an angel from heaven. I won't ask any more. I do not need to ask, I just know you are a special person."

Sir Anthony hailed a hansom cab, handed Abigail in and climbed in beside her. A smell of mould and leather musty with age, along with the strong smells from the street, horse manure, rotting vegetables and too many people.

"Savile Row, and be quick about it."

"Sir." The driver touched his hat with his whip, flicked the reins and the horse set off at a fast pace, weaving in and out of the traffic.

"Damn trams shouldn't be allowed, blocking up the road and as for the peddlars ... "

"You'd have them all removed from the street."

"Of course I would!" Sir Anthony fairly bristled with righteous indignation, and then softened as he saw her smile.

"It is not every day I get to take a beautiful lady to my club. What will they make of you?"

"I thought ladies were not allowed in clubs, Sir Anthony."

"Oh, I just plan to stand at reception until a room becomes available. Everyone can have a look before we go up." He patted her hand. "That is what you want?"

Abigail blushed and looked down, as flirtatiously as she could. Was it that obvious? And seriously, what did she want, the standing on view to everyone to be admired or the going up? Or both?

It seemed no distance at all to Savile Row where she was helped from the cab, her silks rustling around her silk-clad legs, silk on silk, susurrating as she moved. She was aware of the sensuous quality of her dress, and knew Sir Anthony was, too.

The club was elegant, sombre with oak panelling and discreet glass light fittings, with guests who lowered copies of The Times and looked incredulously at the woman clutching Sir Anthony's arm. Abigail could almost hear the startled murmur which ran round the members like a plague of Chinese whispers.

"Sir Anthony." The man behind the reception desk bowed slightly and waited for a command of some kind. He didn't bat an eyelid at Abigail's appearance on Sir Anthony's arm. No doubt he had seen it all before.

"Is there a vacant room, Thomas?"

"There is, Sir Anthony." He reached for a key hanging from the row of hooks on the black wood pigeonholes behind the desk. "You know the way, I think," which told Abigail Sir Anthony had done this before. Perhaps not taken someone out of a Society lunch, though! Well, it had given Myrtle something to talk about for the next few ... years?

The stairs were silent, not a creak of ageing wood gave away their presence. Abigail felt herself going wet with anticipation. Oh make him good, make him strong, make him last!

And for the sake of my peace of mind, make this the room where the mirror hangs!

A room as dark panelled as the rest of the club, thick with long-pile carpet, rich with beautifully carved furniture and a very large bed. It had the emptiness only hotel rooms can have, no personal belongings, nothing that was not strictly useful and cold. A faint hint of lavender and beeswax polish hung in the dust motes. But what mattered was the ornate mirror over the empty hearth. Abigail shivered, as much with relief as with the chill which pervaded the room.

"You seem cold, my dear." Sir Anthony walked over, put his arms around her shoulders and pulled her close. "You temptress, you! Did you believe I did not notice you there and was hoping you would approach me?"

"I had ... an idea," Abigail lied softly, fingering the diamond stick-pin in the cravat and the thickness of the broadcloth jacket. Money spoke to her as much as breeding. If only there was a way of taking money back with her, all her financial problems would be at an end. I wouldn't have to write the book to make money, she thought, smiling softly.

They sat on the end of the bed, arms around each other, Sir Anthony gently exploring the full softness of her cleavage, his fingers touching the nipples which came erect, then sliding between the two mounds. Abigail ran her fingers round his face, traced his jawline, teased and tantalised with her tongue.

"Are you cold?" he looked at her with a quiet, almost loving smile. Abigail took it as an opportunity to get him moving further end faster.

"Well, yes, I am."

"There is one way of making you warm." Before Abigail could blink, he had somehow slipped an arm around her waist, lifted and put her across his knees. Her silks were being dragged back, her silk briefs pulled down. In a flash she had a vision of Lord Danverson, realised this was another man who took pleasure in hurting women. And he held her so tight, there was no escape. She lay staring at the turkey-red carpet, still marked by their footprints, wondering if he would hurt as much as Lord Danverson, and what she had written across her; along with the 'I want sex' message she knew she radiated, was there also an invitation to subdue her?

The pampered soft white hand slapped down again and again on her cheeks. It stung in a different way to her birching, and she screeched, struggled and fought but to no avail. Sir Anthony knew what he was doing. Eventually she gave up fighting, just absorbed the rain of smacks, heard his grunts of pleasure, fought her tears and felt the burning turn to a fiery pain that went deep into her and seemed to sear her clear through to her pussy. I will not cry! she told herself, feeling her face go red in perfect unison with her bottom. She bit her knuckles as the fusillade continued, loud smacks echoing even in the fabric-rich bedroom. In a desperate attempt to displace the pain she wiggled her legs furiously and beat at the bed with her free arm. Sir Anthony laughed and continued spanking her. She realised that from his perspective her pink-shading-to-red buttocks would be joggling about nicely above her silken undies and he would be able to see her pussy lips pouting from between them and her stockinged thighs would be scissoring helplessly. A sight to inflame any man predisposed to hurting women.

After what seemed an eternity, he allowed her to slide to the floor, offered her a hand and pulled, so that Abigail found herself lying flat on her back on the bed, bright-eyed, red faced and out of breath. Beneath her, her buttocks throbbed and stung against the counterpane. That was not like Lord Danverson's birching, but bad enough, thank you! What is it with men lately? What's wrong with good old-fashioned fucking? Abigail tried to sit up but found she was being pushed down again.

Sir Anthony leaned his sleek silver head close to hers.

"Now, are you warmer? Good, in that case it is time to do this."

He sat by her side, and gently stripped off the lilac silk, letting it fall, touching the silk-soft breasts, admiring the plucked pubis with an eyebrow raising smile, of pleasure? Abigail allowed his fingers to wander until finally he let them slide inside the moist, waiting, hot body. His thumb found her clit, rubbed and teased, his other hand staying firmly on a breast, as if trapping a warm small animal in his palm.

"Oh yes, oh yes." Abigail writhed and moaned against the fingers, aware of the burning, aware of the contradictions, loving it. "Please, please..."

But he did not do what she expected, strip off his clothes and enter her to send her to the heights only a real and all-encompassing orgasm could reach; instead he moved around and slipped his thumb firmly between her scalded cheeks. She arched up off the bed in shock. It was always the strangest feeling, not unpleasant exactly but she immediately wanted to move her bowels just as her body was adjusting to having her back passage entered and filled. He pushed in further causing even more havoc inside her, she moaned and twisted but then one finger closed on the sensitive button of her clit, and Abigail came in a series of violent gasping orgasms that swept through her. She closed her eyes and gave herself over to the sheer love of it.

And opened her eyes to find Sir Anthony still neatly dressed, sitting smiling at her.

"Now you can pleasure me." He helped her sit up and opened his fly. He was erect but not very firm. Abigail leaned forward, took him in her mouth, tasted the salt, licked, teased and worked on him. Even though he was not fully erect, it was a fair sized cock and Abby felt it nearly fill her mouth. She rolled her tongue lasciviously around the helm and flicked it at the sensitive spot on the underside – where the foreskin gathered but nothing happened. She reached with one hand into his trousers and cupped the heavy balls but they wouldn't tighten as they normally did when she stroked and sucked a man simultaneously. Miffed now, Abby made some vigorous nodding motions with her head, trying to fool the recalcitrant cock into thinking it was fucking a vagina but she added a few strokes of her tongue up and down the meatus as she did so, a bonus that usually had them spurting thick ropes of sperm into her mouth – if she had decided she wanted to go that far. However, Sir Anthony merely sighed a few times, stroked her head and finally tugged at her curls.

"Don't worry, my dear, you gave me much pleasure."

"But I failed you."

"No, you did everything I expected. Shall we go?"

She dressed in the whispering silk, and slipped an arm through his.

"Did I really please you, Sir Anthony?"

"Oh yes, my dear, you pleased me, but it is a point of principle with me that I do not bed wanton women. I do not know what diseases you might have that I would unknowingly carry to my dear wife, whom I love despite all appearances to the contrary. Here." He threw a couple of gold coins on the bed and stood up. He repeated: "You gave me a lot of pleasure."

Abigail silently scorned his efforts to make impotence seem like a virtue and edged closer to the magic mirror; her passport to freedom and her future, as if she needed to check her rich black curls. But she hesitated. She had to ask.

"Why did you spank me? What did I do wrong?"

Sir Anthony paused in the act of buttoning up his broadcloth jacket and smoothing it over his ample girth.

"Why, nothing, my dear: why do I need a reason to do what I like best? And you know, some women do like it, actually ask for it! Come, we must go. My wife will wonder where I am."

And I wonder where I've heard that before, thought Abigail. "First let me check my hair." She glanced into the mirror ...

Chapter 8: Now

There was a single violet petal crushed in her corset. Somehow, when hurrying back into her clothes, the better to make her escape, Abigail had managed to catch one petal in the folds. It lay in her hand, dried black, almost powdery. It was the first time she had brought something back, something that she could hold in her hand and look at.

She prayed it couldn't do anything to the laws which governed her travelling!

Her Bible lay in her bedside cabinet drawer, carrying its message of love from her grandmother, and the year: 1955. Never read but treasured all the same. Abby slipped the tiny crumbling petal into the pages and put it away. What laws of time travel stopped her going back to see her much loved grandmother once again? What stopped her doing so many things she would like to do: like not throwing away much-loved toys and books, or storing things in the loft so they would be available to be sold for a lot of money today?

She didn't know, and didn't think she would ever find out.

Standing under the shower, letting the hot water trickle down over her body, watching bubbles slide towards her thighs, Abby wondered why she felt good. Sir Anthony had been a disappointment, he had looked strong, he could have gone on for ages, just what she wanted, instead he chose to finger-fuck her and allow her to do a blow job on him, to use crude terms for what had just happened in the club bedroom.

She remembered the odd feeling of helplessness and submission when lying over his knees, awaiting what she knew would be a painful spanking, remembering the glow, the burning, the sensation which somehow transcended the pain and became pure pleasure.

A new experience, one she had, in retrospect, enjoyed.

She grinned suddenly, showing even white teeth in the steamy bathroom mirror.

What would Lord Danverson think of that?

CHAPTER 9: NOW

"Open a new file please, Abigail: Mrs. Lucinda Dawson-Page, matrimonial. And a letter: Mrs. L. Dawson-Page, The Pines, Danverson Lane, Corham, Nr Walchurch - "

Abby took the earphones out of her ears and laid them on the desk, hearing Mr. Wilkins still murmuring on, his tiny tinny voice coming from a great distance. She felt as if she was going to faint, blamed the heat, snatched her foot from the pedal and pressed both hands to her eyes.

Danverson Lane.

Why had it never occurred to her that the Danversons might have been a big enough family to be remembered around here?

And why oh why hadn't she thought about the castle existing somewhere, somehow, even in memory?

August pressed against the windows, sultry hot, threatening thunder. Brooding midges swarmed and danced in thermals that no one but they could feel. The spider plant hung lifeless in its pot. Abby made a mental note to get some water for it when she went to the Ladies.

Danverson Lane.

The Danversons were remembered.

Someone might know where and how and who.

If nothing else, I'd like to know the name of the man I bedded! Lord is nice, but not as a first name, surely!

Come on, she told herself briskly, heat or no heat, August or no August, you have work to do!

She opened a new file and put into it the notes Mr. Wilkins had taken during his interview. Abby lingered over the name of the man involved, Jefferson Nathaniel Stewart. Damn it, was he tall and blond? She couldn't ask outright. Mrs Dawson-Page had enough mysteries to cope with as it was!

The real problem was that Abby couldn't just meet Mrs. Dawson-Page in reception and say: 'You think you know me because we talked together at a midsummer ball in Castle Danverson in June 1625; we talked of Lord Danverson's prowess with the falcon and in bed. Or at least you said he wasn't for you because he was a cruel man with a taste for hurting women. You were right. And you went off with a tall blond man in a green doublet encrusted with gold.'

The dress you wore was a gorgeous thing in blue and gold.

And if your today smile is like the one you turned on me when you met me at the window, no wonder Mr Jefferson Nathaniel Stewart is taken, smitten - nay dying - with love for you!

Mrs. Dawson-Page would not believe it. Abby had difficulty believing it herself.

The tiny Ladies' room encompassed just enough space for three people, assuming one didn't mind being crushed against the wall where the sanitary-towel dispenser lived. Sue lit a cigarette and puffed smoke towards her reflection, pulling all sorts of sultry faces. Linda laughed and Abby grinned, more in companionship than any genuine amusement. She had her fill of smoke in the Hall at Danverson Castle; it had seemed to cling to her hair for ages.

"Heard about that Private Shop opening up in town?" Linda pulled a few strands of mousy brown hair down around her ears and studied her image carefully.

"What Private Shop?" Sue dispensed more smoke efficiently; she was the only seasoned smoker among them. Everyone hated it but Sue had been there so long she was part of the furniture, she came along with the fixtures and fittings.

She was also the only one who could cope with Mr

Brooks' erratic dictation and filing habits.

"Down King's Road, back of the theatre. You know, way out of the main centre. Private Shop, you know, blacked out windows, the whole bit."

"Sounds interesting," Abby made an effort to join in the conversation, but her thoughts were going wildly in all directions. Ever since she had been back from Lady Myrtle's soiree, her thoughts had been going like a hamster on a wheel: round and round the subject of the pleasure she had felt (afterwards), Sir Anthony's admission that some men just like to hurt women - and that some women seem to like it. Apparently she was one of them. Now there was the new twist, the Danverson family, adding to the treadmill of thoughts that refused to go away. Evening classes. Bound to be some evening classes in archaeology, or local history or something! I can find out more! It's August, they start in September, I'd better get a move on!

"Ah, Sister Abigail, the Private Shop is not for you!" Sue winked and made a lewd gesture. "It's for us ladies who know what to do with what God gave us!"

"That's not fair," protested Abby, laughing against her will. "I do know what I've got!"

"But has anyone got close? What about the handsome and tempting Kenneth Thompson then? Him of the BMW and flash lunches? Hasn't he tried to get past the petticoat line?"

"As it happens, no." Abby knew she had a reputation for virtue among the other girls, and also knew they weren't quite at ease with her.

If only they knew what I really do at night, when they all lie sleeping in their beds! If only they knew what adventures a girl can have with a mirror and a micro-second time lapse!

"Anyway, you ought to go along, Abby.' Linda dabbed

mascara at the overloaded lashes which were already threatening to pull her eyelids shut with their weight. "You might find out what it's really like!"

"Might just do that."

"Bet you don't!" Sue stubbed out the cigarette, looked at her watch and pushed herself away from the wall. 'Oh, let's go, time to get back to the grindstone. Muddy Waters is loading me down with urgent stuff today. Why does everyone want to move at the same time, that's what I want to know!"

A Private Shop will have magazines.

The thought came unbidden as Abby climbed back up the ancient stairs, holding on to the wooden handrail.

A Private Shop will have magazines that will tell me why men like giving pain.

Sir Anthony liked it, he said so. He didn't need a reason. He said so.

The 1625 version of Mrs. Dawson-Page said much the same thing. And he did too. Like it - and hurt.

Her phone rang as she reached her office. She picked it up more or less on automatic pilot.

"Abigail, could you bring me the file on the accident at the sawmills? It's not here, so you must have it. And ask Jane to make some tea for Mr. Donaldson and myself, could you?"

"Yes, Mr. Wilkins," Abby rang downstairs and asked Jane for the tea, then retrieved the sawmill accident file from the pile on her floor. She tapped gently on Mr Wilkins' door, went in - and nearly dropped the file.

Mr. Donaldson was Sir Anthony, right down to the gold chain holding in the ample paunch.

She handed over the file and hurried out, her heart hammering against her ribs as hard as it could, physically hurting her. She sank down on her chair and let it spin round, crashing her knee against the desk, not noticing the sharp shard of pain that flared behind her eyes.

Did everyone in the past have their double here today? Everyone and everyone and everyone? If so . . .

If so, what? Time travel is *so* complicated, so confusing and bewildering, there's so many things I don't understand.

"Abby, have you got the pink tape -" Linda broke off, looking at her with concern. "You all right? You look as if you've saw a ghost on the stairs!"

Abby laughed, a little shakily. She had seen a ghost, but not one that Linda would understand.

"I'm all right. I spun my chair around too fast and hit my knee on the desk. It took my breath for a moment." She showed Linda the fast-rising bruise and red mark.

Linda tutted. "I'm always doing that. You must be more careful."

"Pink tape? Yes, it's over there, on the filing cabinet. Can't think why it's over there."

"Thanks, Ab. Put some cold water on that knee."

"Might just do that."

But Abby didn't move, just sat staring at her screen.

Mr. Donaldson was Sir Anthony. She never did find out Sir Anthony's last name, but she'd lay odds it was Donald or Donaldson or some form of it.

Spooky.

Spooky, because in all the times she had been travelling - she always thought of it as travelling - it hadn't happened.

Let's think now. Abby pulled an A4 pad toward her, picked up a ballpoint and began to make notes. This will help with the book anyway, which I am going to write!

There was the guy in the Roundhead camp, somewhere around Dane House, the stately home on the edge of Walchurch. He'd been strong and hard and ridden her

49

for an hour or more until she had screamed in ecstasy. She had hoped for a Cavalier and got a Roundhead instead in every sense of the word! But it had been good and hard and satisfied her for all of a week, until the itch started again, the one that would not be satisfied with an orange vibrator and a bit of KY jelly.

Gamekeeper, real Lady Chatterley stuff that had been: tweeds, smell of heather and woodland and hint of wood smoke and outdoors, a man with a grim face and hard hands which probed and touched and delighted until she had begged for release and found it in a long rough ride that almost the best she'd had.

Georgian lord in his magnificent bedroom, four-poster bed hung with muslin and lace, scent of lilac drifting through the windows, sound of hounds somewhere across the fields, wailing of the huntsman's horn while his horn grew hard and long and delicious and they played 'hunt' all round the large bedroom until he found her hiding place and sank deep into her.

Tudor priest, not one with a conscience, who secreted her in the secret chamber and used her secret chamber for his own communion for several hours, until she could no longer keep his spirit awake and alive, and reluctantly used the mirror in his elaborate quarters to return to the present.

The pub! That had been an oddity. The mirror had transported her to a dark and evil-looking pub, its only shining light the mirror behind the bar. 1910, shabby workmen, but one had taken an instant liking to her. Shabby or not, he had produced a roll of notes from his back pocket and offered her any amount of it she wanted if she would go in the back of his brand new van with him. She had agreed and they had shaken the van's suspension for half an hour until his blackened teeth and foul ale-smelling breath drove her finally to say she was sore. But he seemed pleased enough with his ride, especially when she refused to take the money from him.

But none of them had been here, in the Now that was Reality.

It had changed since the new element had crept into the travelling. Whatever the new element was.

That, she decided, determinedly putting the earphones back in, is something I'm going to check out.

As soon as I can.

CHAPTER 10: THEN

A courtyard, paved and cobbled glowing with golden gaslight. Stained-glass windows of a huge bulking church crowded one side, while the steamy windows of a restaurant kitchen - a closed and shuttered sandwich bar - created a second. On the third were the dark walls of offices closed for the night, all commerce and wheeler-dealing done for another sixteen hours, all this shutting out the noise, clamour and people of Gracechurch Street.

The City of London at night, when everyone had gone, leaving only the cats, rats and City folk who could afford to stay here, the homeless ragged ones found doorways and shelters among the stones and porches.

The gaslight shone on Abigail, stiletto-heeled boots in danger of being trapped in the flagstones and cobbles, fishnet stocking seams straight, short skirt tight, sweater even tighter. Black hair straightened and swept into a smooth face-shaping bob, large chunky plastic earrings and huge bangles, white lips and black-lined eyes.

The fourth side of the square was part alleyway leading to offices and the outside world, and part ancient inn. Through the dim windows, shaded lights lit tables enriched with rum and ale, and worn steps led to richness and seclusion, to scents of spirits strong enough to create a hangover on their own. Red lamps hung over the bar, and a mirror dull and dusty, reflected half-empty bottles with unreadable labels. The timbers of the bar were encrusted with centuries of dirt and dust, sweat and fumes. Three or four men brooded over half-empty glasses, men with thoughts that weighed as heavy as the years on the inn itself.

Abigail walked carefully down the treacherous steps, raising eyebrows and the spirits of the drinkers immediately. She perched - with difficulty - on a bar stool and put the small plastic bag down on the counter.

"Rum and lime, please." She found a couple of ten shilling notes, not sure how much the drink would be. She had decided to actually take something, just to see what happened. Surely one drink wouldn't damage the fabric of time?

"On the house." The barman, leering under shaggy eyebrows which seemed strong enough to stop an avalanche, pushed the drink at her. The glass was smeared, the drink strong.

"Thank you! What have I done to deserve this?" Abigail fluttered mascara-heavy false eyelashes at him and sipped the drink.

"Trade's bad this evening - you've brightened the place up a bit." The bar was wiped with a cloth as dirty as the wood, by hands as large as mooring posts, arms thick as cables. A strong bulky man, ex-sailor? Tattoos shouted he might well be. Face carved from the same wood figureheads were carved from, unreadable eyes topped a large nose. "Waiting for someone?"

"Not really." Every ear was turned her way, every man lusting after long legs that ended somewhere around her shoulders, shiny boots catching the soft light from the bar lamps and the thoughts of the men. "Just not in a hurry to go home. No one to go home for!"

"Shame, nice girl like you." A well-dressed businessman, slim, with groomed blond hair and groomed smooth face, monogrammed briefcase and silk tie, rose from a dark corner where he had been out of her sight. "Could I buy you another drink?"

Abigail hesitated. Who had the mirror to take her back? And who - of this mixed bunch - would provide the spice she had come looking for: a different experience.

One she had read about in the magazines from the Private Shop somewhere in the future: magazines she would never have dreamed were being published anywhere by anyone. But which had touched a chord in her so deep she had come deliberately, provocatively, looking for someone.

Anyone.

Only two men were close, the others ogled from a distance. So, she had to choose between these two.

Choose!

The barman wore a belt strong enough to anchor the Queen Elizabeth but would he use it?

The businessman had no visible sign about him to shout 'I'm the one!'

Abigail took a chance, accepted the offer of a drink with a smile and a nod, and let the magazine she was holding unroll onto the counter. The spanking magazine she had bought from the news-stand in Fleet Street, standing firm and blush-free under the lustful leer of the news vendor and handing over a green note that felt crisp and strange in her fingers. The same magazine she had so carefully concealed as people hurried home, lemmings heading for the station, blindly following their feet and seeing nothing - or did they? A hand swinging nonchalantly at a side would sometimes connect - oh so briefly - with a sensitive area, and then the man would pass on as if nothing had happened, leaving her tingling. And him? She would never know. Another would brush a breast and smile apologetically, but with lustful eyes.

Everywhere the eyes. Eyes on mini-skirts, on what is revealed by mini-skirts, on legs and thighs and twinkling knickers here and there where someone had refused to go into tights, that all-concealing and all-protecting garment.

Carried the magazine, read it over coffee at a stall

while pretending to be homeward-bound, entering Fenchurch Street Station with its smell of trains, of steam and grit, of oil and steel, working men and passengers, of pigeons and people; pretending to queue for the phone, impatiently looking at her watch and rushing away when she was third from the phone box. Who would she call? Her earlier self?

Carried the magazine until the right moment when it unrolled itself on the bar top. Just to see what happened, to see who stiffened, who leered, who went wide-eyed with lust. She'd take a chance on the mirror. It hadn't failed her yet. Neither moved, flicked eyelids or smiled.

Choose!

She chose the businessman, only because of the two he looked cleaner and nicer. She leaned closer, touched his arm, engaged him in conversation, drank her drink and smiled until he said: "Shall we go?"

"Your place?"

"My place."

Silent streets touched by moonlight and lamplight, carrying the echoes of feet and bodies of the day, the hustle of cars, shouting for taxis, calls of news vendors: 'News 'n ' Standard!'

"Here." His place was a top-door flat, up rickety wooden stairs that broke every fire rule she had ever known. Boots clicked on worn wood, heels caught in worn carpet, she stumbled, fell, caught by arms which were strong, breath that carried the scent of whisky and soda. A sudden soft feeling on her ear, on her neck, sending her into acute anticipation that was almost as sharp as her curiosity.

"Here" was a cosy warm place with plump cushions and over-stuffed sofa, turkey carpet and red drapes. Bottles glinted in light dripped by sconces on walls painted with warm-toned emulsion and hung with watercolours and the occasional fine line drawing.

No mirror. Check bedroom.

"What's your name?" Finally asking, after inconsequential chat all the way to the flat.

"Abigail. What's yours?"

"Nigel." It would be, he was a City person after all. Harrys and Bills don't live in City flats.

"Hi Nigel, nice to meet you."

"You're not from round here."

"No, I live in Walchurch."

Not a lie; she did live in Walchurch and it existed for all time, after all. "I just didn't feel like going home tonight."

"Who's waiting for you?"

She turned up her nose. "Mum and Dad, but they don't care much. Mum'll be at Bingo and Dad'll be on the allotment with his mates."

"What, now?"

"Well no, not now, he'll be at The Cricketers by now."

"So you have a little while."

"So, what are we waiting for?" He flopped onto the sofa beside her, one hand sliding the full length of her thigh, finding the bare flesh, slipping two fingers behind the cotton panties, finding the moist slit almost immediately. She gasped and moved, rolled to let him have access.

"You left your magazine behind, but with my loving you won't want that extra stimulus, will you?"

Damn, I chose wrong.

But he might be good.

She pulled him close, let her tongue rove in his mouth, tasting whisky and man, let one hand get busy curled around his cock, feeling the length, the weeping head, running her thumb over the top, pushing back the foreskin, cupping his balls, while the other hastily tugged at her clothes, with his help. His kisses were passionate, his lips firm, his tongue adventurous. Hands touched breasts, neck, thighs, everywhere at once, touching, demanding, seeking out her erogenous zones and caressing them when she reacted.

Clothes were removed in haste as they struggled to free themselves of clinging fabrics, rushing back to kiss as soon as the clothes were dumped unceremoniously on the floor. They were all but naked in front of a two-bar fire which gave nothing back but their slightly misted reflection. Abigail caught sight of Nigel's bronzed body (did he work out and go on holiday a lot?) on her white one and wondered afresh at the exciting contrast.

"Now, now," she panted feeling his fingers become more urgent as his own need stiffened harder and harder. Deep thrusting, pressing her against the carpet, prickles in cheeks against backs of thighs and the weight of a body. She closed her eyes and gave herself over to the sheer intoxicating pleasure of being soundly and completely fucked by a man whose cock filled her to the very limit, pressed against her sides, excited her clit...

"Oh oh, oh." A series of tiny cries which made him laugh just a little. Coming together in an explosion unusual for two people coming together for the first time.

"You're good," he commented as she lay lethargic and limp on his floor. He traced a finger the length of her body, stopping at the nipples and navel, at the pubis now wet and trickling cold.

"I like to think so. You are, too."

"I hope so. I've had enough practice. Now tell me, you didn't miss a bit of spanking, did you?"

"No," she lied. She got up slowly, trailing disappointment behind her. "Could I use your bathroom?"

"Sure, through there. Coffee?"

57

"No, thanks. I must get going."

A quick peek in the bedroom as she passed - no mirror. Damn. I have to go back to the inn.

Hot water and a sponge, highly scented soap that made her nose wrinkle. She had a quick wash down, his sponge where his fingers had been, and dressed again. Time to go.

He was waiting for her by the door.

"Can I see you again, Abigail?"

She smiled, hesitated and then kissed him.

"Look, if I'm at the inn when you are, we'll make it again. How's that?"

"Great. I'll look in after work for you."

"I'll see what I can do." She smiled, kissed him again. "Bye, Nigel, and thanks, It was good." She went down the stairs, mentally going over her route hack to the inn.

Darkness pressed down, streets sounding even emptier than they did before - even the echoes had boarded trains and left for the suburbs. The moon hid its face behind a tumble of curls masquerading as clouds. And the inn's light shone warm and inviting on the worn stones paving the square.

The barman looked up as she clicked dawn the steps, grinned beneath the huge nose and held out her magazine.

"I saved it for you."

"Thank you!" Abigail took it, glanced around the inn and found it empty except for memories. She looked at the man again.

"Come back for what you really wanted?" he asked, touching his belt oh so casually. She shivered, and felt herself melt just a little, anticipation surging through her cheeks and into her spine. Why did it do that?

"Yes." Spoken in the tiniest of voices, unwilling to admit it was what she had come back for, in every sense of the expression.

But she had.

"I could've told you he'd be no good. These white-handed namby-pamby men don't understand what a woman really wants, do they?"

"You're an expert, are you?" she smiled, sliding onto the bar stool, feeling the seams of the short tight skirt almost creak under the strain. She felt completely at home, safe, more secure than she had with Nigel. The mirror must be here somewhere.

And he was offering what she really wanted.

"I'm an expert. Mind you, I don't often find women coming in blatantly asking like you did. Bit of a surprise, that, but I like boldness in a woman, saves a lot of time and trouble." He glanced at a huge watch almost hidden in the hairs of his wrist. "No one's gonna come by now. I'll lock up and we can go."

"I don't ... want to deprive you of trade."

Hesitating, delaying, anticipation building. A belt. She'd not had a belt. It could be dangerous, it could be painful, it could be -

Wonderful.

"To hell with it, it's my pub, I'll do as I damn well wish, and it ain't every day woman comes parading her, half her arse on display, asking for it to be tanned. Come on."

She stood by the bar, waiting, while the huge old door was locked and bolted, lights were switched off, keys hung from a large hook and her arm taken to guide her up the stairs.

More stairs. All she had done that evening was climb stairs, up and down. These held the smell of spirits and age, of dust and good drinking sessions. They by-passed the lounge, she noted, straight for the bed. No messing around here, no coffee and drinks, just -

59

A huge chamber that held an old bed sagging heavily in the middle, and there was the mirror, as out of place as she would be in her current outfit in the offices of Brooks, Wilkins & Co.

"Well, my fine lady, what is it you'd like? What would please you the most, I wonder? A taste of leather, a touch of hand?"

Abigail smiled as softly as she could while inwardly quaking, longing to submit completely to this man, this dominant man, but still holding back just a little.

"Sir, I am in your house, I am at your mercy. Do with me as you would."

His eyes gleamed with barely contained lust.

"Lie down. Face down."

"Shall I ... " She gestured at her clothes.

"No, just lie down." His bands went to the huge buckle on the belt, undid it, began to slide it carefully through the loops.

Feeling vaguely foolish, used to being loved, kissed and possibly undressed before any activity, Abigail took off her long boots and lay down on the bed, pressing her face into the coverlet, uncaring of her eye makeup and bright red lipstick plastering everywhere. That was his problem, not hers. Then there was a sound, a movement, a thrill of air, and she was stung by something which hurt so much her head flew back in astonishment.

"Ah, that's more like it. Reaction at last. You felt that, didn't you?"

Again the belt descended, catching her across the top of the thighs, bringing a shriek to her lips. She tried to roll over, but he pushed her down with one large hand.

"You'll lie there and you'll take it, my girl. You asked for it, and damned if you ain't gonna get it!"

Through her clothes, through her inadequate clothes, the leather bit hard, sending bands of fire through her, nerve ends shrieking in pain. She had never dreamed it could be so hard and heavy, it was almost as if each lash was a punch and in its wake she could feel her buttocks tremble and wobble before they resumed their normal shape and waited for the next one. She clutched the coverlet with both bands, bit it, moaned, screamed and cried aloud as he brought the leather down again and again.

Suddenly he stopped, ripped her skirt in one swift movement, tearing at her skin with the force of it, tearing the panties, exposing skin which must have been scarlet. Abigail quivered, feeling the pain, the burning heat, the sheer fear which held her face-down not moving, afraid to move, afraid to annoy him, this dangerous man with the power to hurt. And she acknowledged her submission to him, her thrill at submitting to him, the thrill of being dominated so completely.

Somewhere, deep below the pain, the core of her being responded to the whole situation and she almost smiled.

He laughed: "Damned if that ain't the prettiest sight I seen in many a moonlit night!" and the belt came down again, harder than ever, flattening her onto the ancient bed. Tears formed, fell. Black mascara ran down her face and onto the cover.

"Oh no, please no, let me up. No, please, stop ..." An endless moaning litany which he ignored, continuing to thrash her until she found everything going faintly woozy and giddy. Then, mercy of mercies, he stopped. She lay very still, feeling intense pain, burning, nerve ends radiating agony at her, feeling tears spilling hopelessly everywhere, wanting to do no more than lie there and cry herself to sleep. But there was no rest.

"Up on your knees, slut. Come on - all fours, like the bitch you are."

Obediently she obeyed, pulling herself up with a

supreme effort, resting her head on the pillow, her arms at each side, trying to support herself, feeling weak and almost shattered by the pain. She felt the bed move as he climbed onto it, urgent fingers at her slit, the telltale moistness from Nigel and from the experience she had just had, warm and cold together. He moved and then rammed deep into her, making her cry out as his massive shaft speared her to her very limits pushed her sheath wide open as it easily barged its way imperiously into her body.

He was harder, longer and firmer even than Nigel, now nothing but a distant memory of pleasurable lovemaking and gentle hands compared to this man; brute strength and vicious aim with a belt. He gripped her stomach with both hands, brought her burning cheeks back onto his hairy body, and rammed against her time and time again, until her cries became cries of pure pleasure, until she called out to him:

"Yes, yes! Harder, harder!" And he did it harder, impossibly harder, until they collapsed together in an orgasm so big it almost threatened to carry her away.

"Damn me if you ain't the finest bit of arse I've had and seen in a long time." Admiring voice, gentle fingers, burning cheeks.

"I could do with a drink," Abigail murmured into his tattooed shoulder.

"Damn right, I could do with one too. Stay where you are." The bed moved, the floor creaked, and he left the room.

In a moment Abigail was off the bed, snatching up the torn skirt and panties. She threw her bag over her shoulder, rushed to the mirror and looked at her tear-stained mascara-streaked self.

And was gone.

CHAPTER 11: NOW

"Abby, dear, you're walking very stiffly tonight, what's the matter? Is it the costume?"

"No, I - I slipped on a step and sat down hard, damaged my coccyx!"

A ripple of sympathetic laughter ran through the cast. Alfred came forward from the darkness of the amphitheatre and smiled up at her. "So you'll be all right?"

"Of course."

"I have to say the purple suits you, Abby, it goes well with the black hair. And Stevie, you look delicious in the red and black!"

Would anyone believe he had been talking dry facts and figures to Mr. Wilkins that afternoon? No one would, if they hadn't seen it for themselves.

I was walking like this then, thought Abby, retiring to the back of the stage, smoothing the purple folds down over her hips. I took tea in for both of them, he just didn't notice a thing. Here he's a different person.

Stevie did look delicious in the red and black. It was a much better choice for her. The blonde hair shone in the lights, the red brought out her pale skin and the black added drama to her pouting looks. The perfect leading lady.

"Right everyone, places - let's run through it from Scene five."

Shuffling of feet as everyone moved around. Lights dimmed and went up again; Alfred retired into the darkness like a vampire retreating to his coffin come the touch of rose dawn. Abby had no words or entrances to make for a while, so she slipped quietly off stage left, came down the steps and stood in the shadows at the side, out of the way, awaiting her cue.

The theatre was chilly as always. Without an audience, the cavernous darkness held nothing but cold whispers and memories of past productions. You could almost imagine ghosts walking here.

"Okay, people! Action!" Charles, the leading man, strode onto the stage, wearing a dark blue doublet and light blue tunic, sleeves slashed with pale blue ribbon, blue trousers, large boots, huge plumed hat in his hand. Black hair fell round his shoulders (a wig), the Van Dyck beard gleamed in the light (real) and Abby caught her breath. She hadn't seen Charles for a couple of weeks. The beard suited him and reminded her of ...

Lord Danverson.

"So, my lady, it has come to this, has it?"

Above her head the drama went on, lines she had memorised without realising it. Her lips moved silently.

Someone came down the aisle at the side. She turned and caught sight of the caretaker, flashed him a smile and was shocked when he shouted out in surprise.

"What's wrong?" Everyone stopped and crowded to the edge of the stage. The caretaker, a little old man with thick pebbled glasses and bald head, collapsed onto the nearest seat, one hand held approximately over his heart. Abby reached him just as Alfred arrived, half grinning,

half annoyed.

"What's the matter, Jim? Seen a ghost?"

"Damn right, Mr Fitzpaine, I thought this young lady here was the lady in purple what haunts this place!"

Alfred laughed.

"No, that's Abby, our Goodwife Manderson! Oh, I see, Abby was in the shadows there! You'll be all right in a minute." He laughed again and went back to his place. "Old Jim thought Abby was a ghost, that's all!"

Amid the laughter, Abby put her hand on Jim's

shoulder and made him jump again.

"Why did you think I was a ghost, Mr. Melville?"

"It was said by some a lady in purple haunts this place, Miss Abby. Floats around in the shadows like you were there."

"Have you ever seen her?"

"Nah, not till now!"

"Jim, Abby, can we have some silence?"

"Sorry, Mr. Fitzpaine." Jim Melville got up and staggered back into the aisle. He nodded to Abby and clumped out of the auditorium again. Abby took her place, waiting for her cue.

Wondering.

CHAPTER 12: NOW

Sunday was summer-bright but autumn chilled, edging toward September, with a sharp blue sky and clouds so white they might have been rain-washed. An occasional gold leaf drifted past the window. Abby frowned over her typewriter, glancing back at the words.

She had told Kenneth Thompson she was writing a book, but had done nothing more than write a few notes for herself. She had decided it was time to really begin work, to prove she could do it. The thoughts had been bothering her for weeks.

And, like a lot of thoughts, they were best laid to rest as soon as she could arrange it.

The mirror seemed to call me. I had no intention of going in the shop, no intention of pushing past damp mouldering furniture and gewgaws, the cheap gimcracks and mementoes of another time; even possessions from a few years earlier seem like things from another time when you wander a house-clearance place. Do they come with the smell of mould and damp, poverty and death trapped within the walls? Is it a requirement laid down by the planners that the place should smell and look like that?

For whatever reason, they all seem the same, and I usually avoid them like the proverbial plague. But the mirror called me.

It was behind a tattered dirty screen, hiding itself from the world. I found it by weaving my way through the tables, lop-sided chairs, water-stained upholstery, and then pushing away a large coat rack that threatened to decapitate me. The mirror hung there, reflecting - Nothing. It should have showed me the cheap print opposite, the lady in the garden picking flowers, thatched cottage background, a Victorian printmaker's dream, a reality that never existed.

But it showed me nothing.

I had to have it.

"Damn pleased to get rid of it," the man grumbled, greased-down hair showing a parting sharp enough to cut paper. He looked and smelled like his shop, a house clearance in himself. Had he come with a vanload of furniture one day, and stayed ever since? "Give us twenty and I'll be glad to see it gone."

"Is it an antique?"

"Don't know. Ask the Antiques Roadshow if they comes here again. All I know is, it gives me the creeps. Don't reflect anything, do it?"

"No, it doesn't." And I had the strongest feeling I should not look into it.

Yet.

I moved a picture on the wall of my two-roomed share-bathroom flat, and hung the mirror in its place. The elaborate ornate gilt/gold frame blended well with the warm peachy emulsion I had painted the walls, and didn't look out of place with a relatively modern three-piece suite I'd got cheap from my aunt. I had the distinct impression it would blend in with whatever surroundings it found itself with.

It glowed, softly. And still I didn't stand in front of it.

Not until night time when I put on a Victorian nightdress, all frills and high neck, ruffled cuffs and ribbons. Not me at all. Not modern at all. A copy of a Victorian lady. I put my hair up in a plait and stood in front of the mirror. And in a second - less than that - I was gone.

There was a fleeting sensation of being nothing, and then I found myself in a large overcrowded bedroom hung with red velvet drapes. There was a clutter of china ornaments and the scent of lilies drifted in through the open leaded window. A large dressing table stood waiting. I looked at it with curiosity: rouge, powders, perfumes and potions.

"Oh, there you are." A voice, a man, gold-haired and elegant, smart suit, gold-topped cane. "Bertie said he'd send someone to the bedroom for me."

I had no idea what he was talking about, where I was, or what I was expected to do, but he obviously did. He tumbled my hair round my shoulders as he kissed me, and pushed me back on the bed.

And I knew I wouldn't fight him.

How?

I don't know. There was a sense of freedom somehow, I could make it with this man and -

Never have to see him again.

How did I know this too? How did I know I could look in the mirror and escape when it was over?

And it was soon over, for he'd had too much to drink. The cock wasn't hard enough but it was a reasonable attempt; with lips and fingers and a little coercion we got a semblance of an erection going, a short thrust or two and he was done, tumbled face down on the bed, snoring. I moved him onto his back so he wouldn't suffocate, gathered up my nightdress, glanced in the mirror -

And was back in my room.

And I thought, this is great! This is what it's all about! I can be pure and good in Walchurch, in 1997, and a whore in the past!

My appetite for sex could be satisfied without my getting a reputation. For no matter how hard you try, someone talks. And I had a job to keep, a reputation to secure and parents to keep happy, even if they didn't live in Walchurch and never spoke to me. They would if they heard anything unsavoury! What an opportunity!

Lunch time already! Abby glanced at the clock, shocked at how much time had gone by. She had an appointment that afternoon, a preview of the local history classes, a walk round Walchurch. She had to go, she had to learn as much as she could.

Over lunch Abby thought about her book. It was a bald statement of what had happened, not the romantic story she bad intended it to be. But what could be more romantic than flying back to the past to find sex and excitement? What I'll do is carry on writing it like that, she decided, gathering up the remains of the crispbread and salad lunch, I can add a strange pen name - something elaborate, very Victorian, a distinctly old-fashioned name - and send it off. When it's done. There's a long way to go.

And not much time to get there. The clock showed one thirty. Abby changed swiftly into a pair of tailored jeans, added a tee shirt with an environmentally friendly trendy message and picked up a lightweight cardigan. Her bag was in the lounge. She snatched it up and went out.

The group was meeting at the White Hart, the large pub in the middle of the road; an island in itself, the traffic normally swirled around it. This sunny lazy, end-of-summer afternoon, the town was almost silent, only litter scraped along the ground as it fought its way out of rubbish bins and went dancing around the empty streets. Abby approached the pub, wondering how many people would be on the walk, surprised to see quite a large group there already.

Mrs. Dawson-Page was among them. With a tall gold-haired man on her arm,

Jefferson Nathaniel Stewart.

At the back of the group, in animated discussion with a couple of young girls, was a leering dark-visaged man with arms like mooring posts and heavy tattoos, if not quite as many as the man she had seen, wearing a leather jerkin and a huge belt that would anchor the Queen Elizabeth.

Abby stopped dead, almost hearing her jaw drop in astonishment. First the lady from the ball and her companion, now this man, and - where did the thought come from? - all I need is to see Nigel now. Abby closed her mouth, pasted on a smile and walled toward the group.

Mrs. Dawson-Page nodded to her, leaned towards the man and whispered in his ear. He looked curiously at Abby. She blushed and moved away.

What were they doing here? Did she have to sit with them through the classes?

What about the other man? Had he signed up for the classes? Her thinking was disrupted by their guide hurrying up, a small man wearing an anorak (despite the sunshine) and flannel trousers, thin brown hair blowing in the cool wind, glasses catching the late sun.

"Hello everyone. Nice to see such a large crowd. I'm George Matheson, your guide for the afternoon. Let's start, shall we?"

The group shuffled their way around him, anxious not to miss a word. A car or two went by, a double-decker bus tore words from his lips and cast them wildly into the slipstream. He smiled nervously and started again.

"The pub where we are is an old one, although it doesn't look old from the outside. It's been built and rebuilt on and off since 1705. The coach stopped here on its way to London, picking up mail and passengers. This used to be the very end of Walchurch, apart from the church itself up there on the hill, of course. The town, or village as it was then, stopped here. If you follow me..."

They set off, crossing the now empty road, tracking the course of Walchurch history: here a new shop-front, above it a timbered facade from the 18th century and ancient roof. Here a sign painted on a wall no one had noticed before. Above eye level who sees history?

Dane Park, gifted to the town of Walchurch by a Victorian benefactor and edged with elms and oaks older than the park itself. Dane House, set at one side, was an old people's home now. Once it had been a fine old Georgian budding. Abby felt her head spinning. History crowded in on her. She wondered at her inability to cope with it thrown at her in one go. The man with the eyebrows walked close and kept looking at her, as others did who had come from her past into today.

Sooner or later he would say: "Haven't I seen you somewhere before?" and she would lie and say: "No, how could you?"

They walked back from the park, along a row of elegant houses with Georgian porches and window frames set back from the road, not noticed before. History, history, history. Ancient pub here, no longer standing; ancient pub there, still standing; how many pubs had Walchurch had? Many more than it had left, for sure, and there seemed to be more than enough now!

"Danverson Lane, named for the local lord of the manor many years ago." Danverson Lane, where the Dawson-Page family lived and now wanted to leave (the house was on the market). What would it feel like to live in Danverson Lane, knowing you had fucked Lord Danverson himself!

The man with the eyebrows edged closer. "Haven't I seen you somewhere before?"

"No." Abby walked swiftly in front, catching up with

the guide.

"We'll go to the church next. The Methodist church is relatively new, late 1800s. It's the parish church which holds interest. Any questions so far?"

"Yes," Abby got even closer. "I read there used to be a castle somewhere around here, was there?"

"Not sure what book you've been reading, Miss..."

"Brandon."

"Miss Brandon, an old one by the sound of it! Yes, there was a castle here, many many years ago. It burned down somewhere around 1750, we believe."

"Where was it sited?"

"Right where the King's Theatre is now."

If there was any more commentary about the town, Abby never heard it. Blindly she followed the group into the church, saw the memorials to the town's dignitaries on the walls, vaguely heard the guide say the Danverson Chapel was blocked off for essential maintenance work, and that they couldn't go in there, it was too dangerous. She looked without seeing at the war memorial, read without reading the names of the glorious dead, saw without registering the strange looks Mrs Dawson-Page gave her, saw a hand sneak out to touch her arm and draw back at the last moment. She must look pretty strange if she was causing that kind of attention. They had done a complete circuit of the town.

"Our last call is Dane House. We can't go in, because of the elderly residents - they don't want a bunch of people trekking through! - but we can look through the gates." Dane House, on the edge of the town where she had fucked a Roundhead in a tent, while a battle built up in the nearby field. The Royalists were gathering, he had said, gathering in force, but he wanted to live before he died.

They stared through wrought-iron gates at a gravel

path and fine-fronted mansion house, saw a man strolling across the lawns, a man who looked remarkably like a guy called Nigel who had a City flat and knew how to fuck even if he didn't know how to really treat a girl. Because if you knew she was into spanking, you shouldn't expect her not to want it.

And the man with the eyebrows watched her every move, her every expression, and wondered no doubt why she never spoke another word.

Lucinda Dawson-Page clung to the arm of Jefferson Nathaniel Stewart as if afraid he would take off in a puff of wind. And yes, he did move with the grace of a jungle cat.

At the end of the tour, Abby said her thanks and goodbyes and went home to ponder strange thoughts.

She had visited Danverson Castle to retrieve her dress, wearing a purple dress. The page had seen her go into Danverson's room and never come out again. She would have appeared to be a ghost.

The Castle was where the theatre is now.

The legend had persisted.

The legend she had created.

The theatre had been built in the 1850s. If the guide was right, the site had stood empty for a hundred years. And the legend had persisted for all that hundred years.

Or, her image, the projected image, had hung around all that time, and enough people had seen her to keep the legend alive.

Another crushing thought - the Danversons had been big enough and rich enough to warrant a whole chapel in the church! She couldn't get to see it, but she would, as soon as the work was done, she'd be in there, looking.

In the meantime, there was a book to write, a play to perform, work to do, and classes to attend.

As well as a few more adventures to be had, for sure.

If the book was to be anything, it had to have adventures in it and that meant experiencing a few more.

A thought entered her head, a wicked evil little thought and she laughed aloud.

Well, it would be one way to experience everything, wouldn't it?

CHAPTER 13: NOW

Abby opened the door to Des's ring and was surprised to find a smart-looking Dracula on the doorstep.

"Like it?" He paraded in his evening clothes, scarlet bow tie and cummerbund, eye makeup darkening shadows around his eyes, making them seem larger and deeper than usual.

"Like it," she approved, pulling her robe closer around her. She didn't want to reveal her outfit immediately.

"Hope there aren't going to be too many Draculas." I

In the light of the hall Abby noticed the blood painted on his lips. "No false teeth, then?"

"Couldn't get any, had to settle for the blood instead. Hope it works."

"Looks good. Come in." She led him into the lounge and pointed to the settee. "Have a seat, I won't be a moment."

"What you're going as, then?"

"You'll see." Smiling at his contorted grammar she disappeared into the bedroom, gave her hair another slick with the hairspray and brush, slipped off the robe and looked at herself in the mirror.

A perfect picture of the time she had 'met' Des in the past, except then the skirt was white and now it was red. Everything else, from the sweater to the stockings, was the same.

She took a deep breath end walked back out into the lounge. "Here I am."

"You look -" he broke off, staring wide-eyed, the make-up forgotten, his mouth dropping open. 'I do know you," he said eventually. Abby shook her head, her black hair not moving under the thick layer of lacquer she had put on.

"No, you don't. You've never seen me before. I just remind you of ... something."

"I'm not with you, Abby."

"Don't worry about it." She picked up the plastic handbag. "Shall we go?"

"Sure. You'll knock their eyes out!"

Dancing close to Des, a couple of rum and limes stored safely inside, where they couldn't be knocked over, Abby allowed herself to drift just a little in her thoughts. No one else had come as Dracula, fortunately for Des, and no one else had come as a Sixties Mary Quant girl either. There was a sprinkling of tarts, one vicar, a milkmaid, a sailor - pretty conventional fancy dress on the whole.

Abby kept recalling a magnificent ball, where everyone wore long flowing dresses, doublets, lace and ribbons which fitted them to perfection, because (the key lay in the because) everyone wore that type of clothing all the time, and they didn't move or look awkward in it. Wise Alfred to insist they wore their costumes at home! Not that Abby needed to; she felt more at home in that outfit than any other costume she had ever had and felt herself longing for the midsummer ball, for the smoke and the noise and the ale, for ...

For Lord Danverson to have a hand on the wall beside her, to be talking close into her ear, his Van Dyck beard tickling her face, making her want to reach out and caress it.

But he was then and this was now, and she had a companion she had to be nice to.

She wondered, just for a moment, why the music she was dancing to seemed odd, strange, almost raucous; it was only wallpaper music, for heaven's sake! But hadn't they any minstrel music, lute and lyre?

Come on, she told herself, this is a party, loosen up! But images remained, staying just out of the corner of her eye, the corner of her mind.

Drink had been knocked over, the purple dress would definitely have been a mistake in such a crowded place. The party was to celebrate the engagement of a couple of Des' friends, doing it in style. Des told Abby the wedding would be done in style, too: elegant Victorian dress for everyone, men and women alike, and a horse-drawn carriage for the bride, all planned for May next year. They looked happy enough, dressed in identical pirate outfits, hardly moving from one another's side.

The guests, also Des' friends, welcomed Abby as if they had known her forever. Only one man had become persistent, questioning her at length about the theatre, why the Community Centre should give space over to amateur dramatics.

"People like the plays, it gives us all an interest, it's a good use for a community centre. And we do it for the love of it. Come and see at the end of October. We're doing a play set in the time of Charles I, 'For Glory and For Love.' You'll like it, I'm sure." No, what I'm sure of is that you're pestering me with questions because you don't want me to leave your side. You don't know where you've seen me before, but I do.

She finally walked away with her Dracula, who had been giving the man meaningful angry looks all the time.

"I think he's a reporter of some kind," Des told her as they went into a smoochy dance.

"No, I know the reporters who come around the theatre. He isn't one of those. I think he just likes the legs."

"As I do!"

She didn't tell Des she had seen the man before, in the inn in the City of London when she had walked in here and boldly picked up first Nigel and then Des himself, the barman as he was then, nameless and virile and strong. The man had been sitting by one of the windows, had admired her from a distance, had looked disappointed when Nigel had got to her first, and she had walked off holding Nigel's arm.

She didn't tell him because, like the outfit itself, none of it would have made sense, and yet somewhere in Des' mind then were tiny bells ringing, and he couldn't quite make sense of why they should be making a noise.

They left at 11 o'clock. Abby's feet were aching in the heeled boots and her legs ached from too much dancing. She felt tired, hot and sticky but guessed Des would want to get a lot further than the front door.

"Can I offer you..."

He kissed the back of her neck. "Yes, you can."

She turned and allowed him to take her into his strong tattooed arms, feeling the iron strength, the large hands cupping her cheeks firmly, pulling her hips close to his.

"I've wanted you ever since you walked out of the bedroom wearing that outfit." She kissed him, tongues touching, teeth contacting, lips pressed hard against each other, feeling his incipient stubble. Somehow she dropped the bag onto the settee, somehow they made it to the bedroom, kissing and hugging and touching.

They separated for a moment while Abby took off the high-heeled boots with a sigh of relief, stripped off the clinging top and miniskirt, fell back onto the bed at his touch, and let him remove the rest of her clothing slowly and carefully. She noticed his quick look at the cp magazine on the cabinet, saw him look and then look away, his eyes unreadable. He took time over the suspenders and the fishnet stockings, rolling them sensuously down to her feet, where he touched and caressed and rubbed her high insteps. Then his fingers travelled the length of her legs, finding her silk-soft thighs, her moist opening, her silk-smooth pubis.

"Nice."

She said nothing, just let his fingers walk, closing her eyes, wondering if it would be as good. There were disadvantages in travelling; you always had something to compare with.

Another pause while Des stripped off his Dracula clothes, dropping them in an untidy heap. He was well built, with interesting scars lancing across his chest and stomach; Abby didn't ask, it wasn't the moment. Instead, she traced the silvery red lines with a long fingernail, making him twitch. He was ready, his cock moved of its own accord, seemed to be guided towards her. He slid into her, murmuring, "I've waited long enough," and lay there, letting her experience the fullness, the complete filling of her body. She grasped his shoulders, pulled him close, kissed him. He buried his face in her neck, pretending to bite, scratching the sensitive skin.

"Go!" she whispered, and he began to move his hips, gently, taking his time, each thrust long drawn out and gentle, yet firm. She thrilled to the timing, the movement, the slow tender build-up towards a more frenetic coupling that suddenly exploded.

The springs complained and came back into position as they rolled over, smiling at each other, content with what had happened. Not bad, thought Abby, not bad at all.

Des picked up the magazine with his left hand, waved it at her.

"Into this, are you?" He smiled, but his eyes held no knowing look.

"On and off," admitted Abby, waiting to see what would happen. He flipped the pages and then put it down.

"You didn't need that with my loving."

She wondered where she'd heard something like that before.

"You're good," he said, running a thumb down the length of her body, finding her wet thighs, tickling her tender spots.

"You are, too."

"I hope so, I've had enough practice. Now tell me, you didn't miss a bit of spanking, did you?"

"No" she lied. "Coffee?"

"Fine."

After coffee and more kisses, Abby finally got him to go, watched him walk away into the darkness, closed the door and sank down on the settee.

It wasn't any good. It was like ham without mustard, chocolate without cream, rum without lime. Oh, it had been fine at the time, when it was happening, after it had happened, but then the feeling wore off and there was nothing left but wetness and a sense of disappointment.

What had happened? When had it changed?

From the time she came back from Danverson Castle wearing a hundred red lines which burned and stung and glowed like nothing on earth.

Because Lord Danverson had fucked her first and thrashed her afterwards.

And left her wanting.

Abby stood up, made her way to the bedroom, found the torn white skirt, looked at it, smiled and then went for her sewing box.

CHAPTER 14: THEN

A courtyard, paved and cobbled, glowing with golden gaslight. Stained-glass windows of a huge bulking church crowded one side, while the steamy windows of a restaurant kitchen - a closed and shuttered sandwich bar - created a second. On the third were the dark walls of offices closed for the night, all commerce and wheeler-dealing done for another sixteen hours, shutting out the noise, clamour and people of Gracechurch Street.

The City of London at night, when everyone had gone, leaving only the cats, rats and City folk who could afford to stay here, the homeless and ragged found doorways and shelters among the stones and porches.

The gaslight shone on Abigail, stiletto-heeled boots in danger of being trapped in the flagstones and cobbles, fishnet stocking seams straight, short skirt tight, sweater even tighter. Black hair straightened and swept into a smooth face-shaping bob, large chunky plastic earrings and huge bangles, white lips and black-lined eyes.

The fourth side of the square was part alleyway leading to offices and the outside world, part ancient inn. Through the dim windows, shaded lights lit tables enriched with rum and ale, and worn steps led to richness and seclusion, to scents of spirits strong enough to create a hangover on their own. Red lamps hung over the bar, and a mirror, dull and dusty, reflected half-empty bottles with unreadable labels. The timbers of the bar were encrusted with centuries of dirt and dust, sweat and fumes. Three or four men brooded over half-empty glasses, men with thoughts that weighed as heavy as the years on the inn itself.

Abigail walked carefully down the treacherous steps, raising eyebrows and the spirits of the drinkers immediately. She perched - with difficulty - on a bar stool and put the small plastic bag down on the counter.

"Rum and lime, please." She found a couple of ten shilling notes, not sure how much the drink would be. She had decided to actually take something, just to see what happened. Surely one drink wouldn't damage the fabric of time?

"On the house." The barman, leering under shaggy eyebrows that seemed strong enough to stop an avalanche, pushed the drink at her. The glass was smeared, the drink strong.

"Thank you. What have I done to deserve that?" Abigail fluttered mascara-heavy false eyelashes at him and sipped the drink.

"Trade's bad this evening - you've brightened the place up a bit." The bar was wiped with cloth as dirty as the wood, by hands as large as mooring posts, arms thick as cables. A strong bulky man, ex-sailor? Tattoos shouted he might well be. Face carved from the same wood figureheads were carved from, unreadable eyes topped a large nose. "Waiting for someone?"

"Not really." Every ear was turned her way, every man lusting after long, long legs that ended somewhere around her shoulders, shiny boots catching the soft light from the bar lamps and the thoughts of the men. "Just not in a hurry to go home. No one to go home for!"

"Shame, nice girl like you." A well-dressed businessman, slim, with groomed blond hair and groomed smooth face, monogrammed briefcase and silk tie, rose from a dark corner where he had been out of her sight. "Could I buy you another drink?"

Abigail didn't hesitate.

Only two men were close, the others ogled from a distance.

So, she had to choose between these two.

But there was no choice, was there? Not with knowledge.

The barman wore a belt strong enough to anchor the Queen Elizabeth, and she knew he would use it.

The businessman had no visible sign about him to shout 'I'm the one!' and of course he wasn't.

Abigail shook her head.

"Thank you, but I have a drink already."

The magazine slipped from her fingers and unrolled on the counter. She had carried it so carefully concealed as people hurried home, lemmings heading to the station, blindly following their feet and seeing nothing - or did they? A hand swinging nonchalantly at a side would sometimes connect - oh so briefly - with a sensitive area and then the man pass on as if nothing had happened, leaving her tingling. And him? She would never know. Another would brush a breast and smile apologetically, but with lustful eyes.

Everywhere the eyes. Eyes on mini-skirts, on what is revealed by mini-skirts, on legs and thighs and twinkling knickers here and there, where someone had refused to go into tights, the all-concealing and all-protecting garment.

Carried the magazine, read it over coffee at a stall while pretending to be homeward-bound, entering Fenchurch Street Station with its smell of trains, of steam and grit, of oil and steel, working men and passengers, of pigeons and people; pretending to queue for the phone, impatiently looking at her watch and rushing away when she was third from the phone box. Who would she call? Her earlier self?

Carried the magazine until the right moment when it unrolled itself on the bar top. Knowing what would happen, knowing who would stiffen, who would leer, who would go wide-eyed with lust.

She didn't have to take a chance on the mirror. It was waiting for her upstairs, along with pleasure through pain.

She smiled at the businessman, because of shared memories. He looked puzzled, knew something was wrong but didn't know what. He went back to his table, staring into his drink.

Outside, silent streets touched by moonlight and lamplight, carrying the echoes of feet and bodies of the day, the hustle of cars, shouting for taxis, calls of news vendors.

'News 'n' Stand'd!'

As time went on, the darkness pressed down. Streets sounded even emptier than they did before; even the echoes had boarded trains and left for the suburbs. The moon had hidden its face behind a tumble of curls that masqueraded as clouds. And the inn's light shone warm and inviting on the worn stones that paved the square.

The barman looked at her and grinned. He leaned over the scarred bar top and whispered: "You made the right choice, girlie."

She smiled back. "I know."

"Another drink?"

"Thank you!" Abigail took it, glanced around the inn and found it empty (when had Nigel and the other solitary drinkers gone?) except for memories. She looked at the man again.

"Come back for what you really wanted?" he asked touching his belt oh so casually. She shivered, and felt herself melt just a little, anticipation surging through her cheeks and into her spine. Why did it do that?

"Yes." (How did he know I'd come back?) She spoke in the tiniest of voices, unwilling to admit it was what she had come back for, in every sense of the expression.

But she had.

"I could've told you he'd be no good. These white-handed namby-pamby men don't understand what a woman really wants, do they?"

(But in another time and another place it's you that is no good!)

"You're an expert, are you?" She smiled, shifting on the bar stool, feeling the seams of the short tight skirt almost creak under the strain. She felt completely at home, knowing the mirror was there. Knowing what was on offer. This, then, had been the preview she felt last time.

"I'm an expert. Mind you, I don't often find women coming in blatantly asking like you did. Bit of a surprise that, but I like boldness in a woman, saves a lot of time and trouble." He glanced at a huge watch almost hidden in the hairs of his wrist. "No one's gonna come by now. I'll lock up and we can go."

"I don't ... want to deprive you of trade."

Hesitating, delaying, anticipation building. Delaying for the pleasure of feeling the anticipation build.

She knew it would be wonderful.

"To hell with it, it's my pub, I'll do as I damn well wish, and it ain't every day a woman comes parading in here, half her arse on display, asking for it to be tanned. Come on."

She stood by the bar, waiting while the huge old door was locked and bolted, lights were flipped off, keys hung from a large hook and her arm taken to guide her up the stairs.

More memories.

These stairs held the smell of spirits and age, of dust and good drinking sessions. They by-passed the lounge, she noted, straight for the bed. No messing around here, no coffee and drinks, just -

A huge chamber that held an old bed sagging heavily in the middle, and there was the mirror, as out of place as she would be in her current outfit in the offices of

Brooks, Wilkins & Co.

"Well, my fine lady, what is it you'd like? What would please you the most, I wonder? A taste of leather, a touch of hand?" Abigail smiled as softly as she could while inwardly quaking, longing to submit herself completely to this man, this dominant man, but still holding back just a little.

"Sir, I am in your house, I am at your mercy. Do with me as you would."

His eyes gleamed with barely contained lust.

"Lie down. Face down."

"Shall I ... " she gestured at her clothes.

"No, just lie down." His hands went to the huge buckle on the belt, undid it, began to slide it carefully through the loops. Feeling vaguely foolish, used to being loved, kissed and possibly undressed before any activity, Abigail took off her long boots and lay down on the bed, pressing her face into the coverlet, uncaring of her eye makeup and bright red lipstick plastering everywhere. That was his problem, not hers. There was a sound, a movement, a thrill of air, and she was stung by something which hurt so much her head flew hack in astonishment. (Why don't I ever remember how much it hurts?)

"Ah, that's more like it. Reaction at last. You felt that, didn't you?"

Again the belt descended, catching her across the top of the thighs, bringing a shriek to her lips. She tried to roll over, but he pushed her down with one large hand.

"You'll lie there and you'll take it, my girl. You asked for this and damned if you ain't gonna get it!"

Through her clothes, through her inadequate clothes, the leather bit hard, sending bands of fire through her, nerve ends shrieking in pain. She had forgotten how hard and heavy the belt was, it was almost as if each lash was a punch and in its wake she could feel her buttocks tremble and wobble before they resumed their normal shape and waited for the next one. She clutched the coverlet with both hands, bit it, moaned, screamed and cried aloud as he brought the leather down again and again.

Suddenly he stopped, ripped her skirt in one swift movement, tearing at her skin with the force of it, tearing the panties, exposing skin which must have been scarlet. Abigail quivered, feeling the pain, the burning heat, the sheer fear which held her face-down, not moving, afraid to move, afraid to annoy him, this dangerous man with the power to hurt.

And she acknowledged her submission to him, her thrill at submitting to him, the thrill of being dominated so completely. Somewhere, deep below the pain, the core of her being responded to the whole situation and she almost smiled.

He laughed. "Damned if that ain't the prettiest sight I seen in many a moonlit night!" and the belt came down again, harder than ever, flattening her onto the ancient bed. Tears formed, fell. Black mascara ran down her face and onto the cover.

"Oh no, please no. Let me up. No, please, stop ..." An endless moaning litany which he ignored, continuing to thrash her until she found everything going faintly woozy and giddy. Then, mercy of mercies, he stopped. She lay very still, feeling intense pain, burning, nerve ends radiating agony at her, feeling tears spilling hopelessly everywhere, wanting to do no more than lie there and cry herself to sleep. But there was no rest.

"Up on your knees, slut. Come on - all fours, like the bitch you are."

Obediently she complied, pulling herself up with a supreme effort, resting her head on the pillow, her arms

87

at each side, trying to support herself, feeling weak and almost shattered by the pain. She felt the bed move as he climbed onto it, urgent fingers at her slit, the telltale moistness from Des and from the experience she had just had, warm and cold together. He moved and then rammed deep into her, making her cry out as his massive shaft speared her to her very limits pushed her sheath wide open as it easily barged its way imperiously into her body.

He was harder, longer and firmer even than Des, now nothing but a distant memory of pleasurable lovemaking and gentle hands compared to this man; brute strength and vicious aim with a belt. He gripped her stomach with both hands, brought her burning cheeks back onto his hairy body, and rammed against her time and time again, until her cries became cries of pure pleasure, until she cried out to him:

"Yes, yes! harder, harder!" And he did it harder, impossibly harder, until they collapsed together in an orgasm so big it almost threatened to carry her away.

"Damn me if you ain't the finest bit of arse I've had and seen in a long time." Admiring voice, gentle fingers, burning cheeks.

"I could do with a drink." Abigail murmured into his tattooed shoulder.

"Damn right, I could do with one, too. Stay where you are." The bed moved, the floor creaked, and he left the room.

In a moment Abigail was off the bed, snatching up the torn skirt and panties. She threw her bag over her shoulder, rushed to the mirror and looked at her tear-stained mascara-streaked self.

And was gone.

CHAPTER 15: NOW

The gamekeeper was good.

That was an easy one for me. I found a late-Victorian dress in the theatre wardrobe, full flowing sleeves and long flowing skirt, let my hair hang down in half curls, wore buttoned boots and carried a parasol. Glanced in my magical mirror and was...

In a woodland clearing. Somewhere, a small stream talked to itself as it hurried on its way, passing messages to stones and rushes as it went along. A bird or two called, fluttered, rocked branches. Beetles swarmed over trees, butterflies decorated an afternoon sky, flashing colours on pale blue, rather like the dress I was wearing.

"My Lady, you are out of the grounds of the house."

The man's voice caught me by surprise. Although I was looking for someone, I did not see him among the trees, his tweeds blending so well with the foliage, the brown trunks, the crawling ivy that clung and patterned the bark.

He was a tall, strong man, face browned with rain and wind, sun and snow, neat trimmed moustache, eyes that missed nothing, looked through my clothes as if I wore nothing, as if I were naked in the clearing - as well I might be for all that the world knew of my being there.

"Her Ladyship will wonder where you are," he went on, moving close, almost silently though he trod twigs and branches, dead leaves and debris thrown down unwanted by the forest in which we stood.

"I don't think her Ladyship will miss me." I smiled as best I could, eyeing the body, knowing it was what I wanted. Here. Now. But the ground was rough and my dress might be torn and I would have to explain it away to someone somewhere if I did. "And you are?"

He came closer, put a hand on my arm, a hand

roughened by work and wild life. "Travis, Miss. Her Ladyship's gamekeeper. I was keeping a watch on these woods for poachers, you see."

"I'm no poacher," I laughed quietly, spreading my hands to show I had nothing but a ruffled parasol that would not keep off a raindrop let alone a shower.

"I can see that, Miss."

"So, Travis, what shall we do about this situation in which we find ourselves?" I put my tongue between my teeth very quickly and looked at him with a saucy inviting look. He read the message and flushed just a little.

"That's up to you, Miss."

"Will her Ladyship mind if you don't patrol these woods this afternoon?"

"Her Ladyship never asks what I be about, Miss."

"In that case - "

"It is not often a lady gets to be so bold."

"I know that, but I do not have a lot of time and there are things I want to experience."

He read it the wrong way, as I'd hoped he would.

"Young ladies these days do not get much chance of freedom, it seems to me, never a chance to get out and find out about life and things like that. I understand, Miss. Come with me."

And he set off at a fast pace through the woods, following a track I could barely see. I had to hurry to keep up with him, catching my sleeves on bramble and elder, finding an oak trunk here, an elm there to stop myself from falling. He paid no attention to my stumbling, made no effort to help me through the rough patches.

His cottage appeared suddenly; a magic cottage, a witch's cottage, low-gabled with leaded windows, gloomy porch and a doorway overhung with black bryony in place of roses. A few cabbages and other vegetables studded the neglected flowerbeds, and a rosemary bush leaned sorrowfully to one side. I ran my hand over it, savouring the sharp, piquant scent as we entered.

A man's place: a pipe in a bowl on the table, a tobacco jar, a flint and steel. A tankard on the sideboard a bowl of fruit, none fresh. A few prints, no flowers, no polish, no sense of being cared for.

"Tea?"

"No, thank you."

"Impatient, are you?"

"Sort of." The one thing I didn't know then or now is how long the mirror would let me be somewhere - would it call me back or could I stay as long as I wanted? I hadn't tried to find out.

"The bedroom's through here."

No subtlety here either, just wood-smoke and heather, rosemary on my hands, a man kissing my face and neck in a way no one had done before, lips as hard as the fingers which sought and found breasts, nipples, which caught at the skirt, tore at the petticoats, found my moistness and made me gasp with pleasure.

"I knew you be out looking for sommat, Miss and now you've found it." I tossed the parasol aside and the dress with it, fell back on the bed and let the rough hard fingers, as rough as the bark of any tree I ever touched, find their way in and around my various secret places, revelling in the torment of being brought to near orgasm and allowed to sink back, only to be brought up again and again. I knew not then where he found his expertise, and I did not ask. I would not ask. I loved every moment; no questions asked, no quarter given, none asked or taken.

I said nothing, just grasped him in both my hands,

held him firm, felt the strength, a branch of his own, let him take me, wrapped my legs round his waist and cried out as he thrust; let him turn me over onto all fours, let him take me again and again that way.

I let him drop me, rag doll like, over the side of the bed, exhausted and satiated; let his member slide limp in my hand then played and teased and sucked and kissed and tormented until it rose as strong and fit again as a plant after rain. My answering body, bent over the end of the bed, let him take me in the other orifice, his fingers deep in the front, his cock deep in the back. Could there be such pleasure? Could there be such feelings? Could there be such satisfaction?

"Do you have a mirror?" I asked, wanting to tidy the wayward half curls and straighten my dress before venturing back to the house, wherever it was.

"Here." He took me to the other room where the mirror waited. "Her Ladyship gave it to me, for she said it reflected nothing she wanted to see."

"Thank you." As he turned away, I looked in it ...

I know just how long I am gone each time - less than a second. I know, because the watch I leave on the table begins the sweep of the second-hand as I look in the mirror and has yet to touch the number six before I am back and picking it up again. Less than a second to have hours of pleasure, for a touch of fear that is mustard on the ham, the fear I might not find the mirror, the fear that something will go wrong; it makes the making even more pleasurable. Much more pleasurable. No wonder I find today's lovers so ... dull!

Chapter 16: Now

"A little bird whispered you were partying on Saturday, Abby." Sue smiled knowingly as Abby paused by the secretary's room.

"Yes." Abby went in, leaned against the spare desk, idly pulled the covers into place. "Someone I met at evening classes, his friends were having an engagement party. We went in style, fancy dress."

"So I heard. They said you looked like Mary Quant!"

"I wanted to be Dusty Springfield but I don't have the right colour hair!"

"I said to my friend, you must be wrong, Sister Abigail doesn't go partying!"

"Depends who's asking."

"Certainly must have made an impact," Sue grinned knowingly. "You'll be down the Private Shop next!"

Little do you know! thought Abby, hiding a smile behind a cough.

"What evening classes are those, Ab?" asked Linda, tidying her hair before a tiny square of mirror on the mantelpiece.

"Local history. Thought I'd find out something about the place where I live."

The phone started ringing in Abby's room. She looked ruefully at the two women and went out. So, it had got around already, had it? One party, one night out, and already people were talking! How wise she was to keep her main partying for the past, which was truly another country, where no one knew what went on. Now or then.

Monday morning brought its usual crop of work, divorce problems from the weekend, access orders not adhered to, marital arguments over property flaring up, accidents on the roads, always something happening.

And beneath it all a feeling that she was close to

something, something big, something that would shake her very foundations. Abby wasn't sure where the feeling had come from, but it was there. Waiting. Lurking in the background, waiting to pounce.

She bought sandwiches for her lunch, waited until Linda and Sue went out for a walk in the bright sun, and sat at her machine, swiftly transcribing the typed notes onto disk. Mr Wilkins wouldn't mind, surely he wouldn't. She felt as if she had to have a more permanent record than her papers; what if the flat catches fire while I'm out?

Underneath it ran a different thought, not very often expressed. If I get trapped in the past, if I can't find the mirror, or something goes wrong, I need to leave some other record of where I am and where I might be, and what happened..

Something. Somewhere.

If I get to finish the book, I'll put the disk in the safe.

And she went on to write the next chapter.

CHAPTER 17: NOW

The priest was the biggest surprise of all.

Everyone knows what the Church was like in the Middle Ages, everyone knows about bishops having love-children; heavens, it happens even now, but then it was widespread accepted, usual.

But still, for someone brought up in the Anglican faith where people were loyal to their vows (for the most part) and life on the whole was as you expected it to be, this lover was a shock.

I arrived in a flowing dress of gold-and-russet silk, with high starched collar standing well away from my face which was crowned with combs and a veil. Tight-fitting sleeves flared out from my elbows, gold choker held the collar, and a gold pendant hung at my waist. Elegance, pure exciting elegance. I'd hired it specially from a costume shop. No one in the theatre had such a wonderful dress - we hadn't staged such a performance. I arrived at some kind of musical evening, where musicians delicately plucked lyres and mandolins played plaintive delicate airs that wove themselves in and around the hairs on the back of my neck. I trembled at their touch, as much as I trembled when a man looked at me. I slipped quietly from the gathering between airs, walked the long corridors, admired the tapestries, glowing, rich, beautiful in a way I had never seen them before. I shivered in the cold draughts which came from everywhere and nowhere. It felt like Danverson Castle, and yet ...

"Madam, you are not attending the musical evening?"

A priest, red cloak red clothes, black hat, heavy silver cross, stood staring at me.

"I ... felt a little faint. I sought some air."

"Ah, come with me. I will find you a potion for

faintness that will cure it immediately."

We went to a small panelled room where he pressed a piece of carving and a door slid aside.

"You keep your potions in such a place?" I asked, wondering what he was at.

"Come and find out." He pulled my arm and I could do nothing but go with him.

Inside the tiny space it was dark, very dark.

"My secret priest's hiding hole." He grinned in the darkness, lit a candle. I saw his gleaming eyes. "You are not of the household, nor are you a visitor, my lady. I know not who you are, but I know precisely what you came for."

He was right. Beneath his flowing robes and beneath my flowing dress we had a mutual meeting of bodies, his hard, mine soft, his determined, mine willing, his fingers quick and eager, mine capable of keeping his spirit alive as long as it took. You need little room when your legs are straight up in the air, if someone is holding you against a wall and ramming against you with all their strength and you are doing nothing but gasping in ecstasy, and if you make too much noise a hand is clapped across your mouth. Have you tried to orgasm in silence? It can be done, but it centres your thoughts on one place and one emotion wonderfully...

We rested, we waited we went again; we rested, we waited, we went again and then again.

At last I emerged from his secret hole, tired, shaking, satiated with his juices and my own emotions. I saw the mirror immediately, hanging over the fireplace in which burned a small, sullen fire.

"A moment to tidy my hair," I told him as he pulled at the cloak and straightened his hat.

And no doubt shocked him more than did my sexuality when I disappeared before his eyes.

I wish I'd found out if it was Danverson Castle. It felt like it.

I also wish I knew why I had 'I'm available for sex' stamped all over me in the past, while here I am called Sister Abigail.

Just in time, for there were voices on the stairs, her boss, the client he had at two pm and Jane with tea on a tray. Best be done with such thoughts at work, Abigail Brandon! Back to serious matrimonial problems and road accidents.

Back to the essentials of life.

Yes, but the fucking is my essential of life.

And don't you forget it.

Talking of which ...

She paused, rested a hand on the desk, thought about Des, who had left a message that morning that he would like to talk to her.

Should she see him again, after the disappointment of Saturday night? Could she encourage him to turn her over and spank her, or use that belt he so obviously flaunted at times? Or is it only me who thinks he's flaunting it? To him it might be natural to wear such a belt! It's just that I know different.

Would he do what his predecessor had done - thrash her long and hard and bring her to an orgasm that once she could not have dreamed of!

I thought the priest was good, she reminisced, tapping the disk and then putting it safely in the drawer. I thought the priest was good and the gamekeeper the best ever.

Then I went to the City inn and got belted and fucked.

Damned if that wasn't better than any of them.

Before or since.

But that's for a later chapter.

CHAPTER 18: NOW

In the end it was easier to agree to another date; after all, she would have met up with Des at the evening classes anyway.

"I've given a lot of thought to the other night," he said, leaning closer to her, almost whispering. The Cricketers was crowded. Abby was sure a karaoke evening was about to start up, something she couldn't stand.

"Me, too," she said truthfully, meeting his look. She didn't tell him, couldn't tell him, how she had left her flat and gone back to the old Des, the one with the belt and the ability to bring her to the closest thing to paradise for the few seconds/minutes/eternity the orgasm lasted.

"I think I let you down." He pushed his half pint of lager around on the coaster, watching the movement of the drink in the glass. "I think I should read your books and try to understand."

"It's all right," she said softly, but quivering inside. Yes, yes, yes! screamed her body, her thoughts, her mind. Would they reach him? Even if he wasn't by nature a man who could dominate - an expression she had come to learn through reading her books - he could have a go, and who knew what might happen?

But only a true-born dominant will do, warned a small voice. A man like -

Lord Danverson. Now there was a man. Gave an order and I went running. Before I knew what being a submissive was all about. I left the ball, I went to his room, I waited for hours.

I did what he told me.

Without question.

Because -

"What do you think of the evening classes so far?"

Des abruptly changed the subject as a couple came close, sat down at the next table; cigarettes and lighters, sharp smell of whisky and more delicate scent of sherry and perfume.

"Bit boring," Abby shrugged. "Might get more interesting when we come a bit closer to our time."

And I learn more about Danverson Castle.

"I agree, I don't think I'd bother much, except you're going to be there."

More people crowded in. The noise became overwhelming, cigarette smoke and heat intensified. Abby decided she had enough. She smiled, held out a hand. "Shall we go?"

It was as open an invite as she could give him. With luck, in the subdued light of the shaded lamps of her flat he wouldn't notice the lines left by his ancestor's belt, the deep bruises that throbbed and burned and gave her thrill after thrill, an adrenaline high she rode for the entire night after getting back. Even after his lovemaking she had rolled and writhed around the bed with memories and vibrator slick with her body fluids, thrusting, manoeuvring, hips raised off the bed, head pushed back against the headboard, crying aloud the sounds she had not dared make even while knowing the inn was empty of all but her and the man she had visited. Twice.

And then she slept nearly all of Sunday.

"Sure." Des drained the lager and pushed his way out of the bar, opening the door on the coolness of a late September evening. Dark, yet not quite dark, sun not quite ready to give itself over to the fingers of black which probed and pushed it below the horizon. An owl hooted, a crow called and cawed before settling for the night. Clouds were building, heavy rain clouds belly down with moisture, ready to weep over Walchurch.

"Looks bad," Des commented, pulling his jacket

around his throat. "Let's go!"

But Abby was reluctant to hurry too much, wanting to enjoy the chill, the sense of warmth of the man next to her, his arm through hers, his step matched to her shorter ones. Cars raced by, hyphen of headlight and dash of red before they were gone on whatever errand brought them out into the streets at night: mysterious business or sensible ordinary errands, a mother to visit, a hospital or pub to visit, or just a lonely empty home. Or a loveless one.

My, I'm romantic and spiritual tonight!

In the semi-darkness, the King's Theatre loomed large among the shops and offices, much as the castle must have done so many years before. Lights gleamed in the downstairs windows, where the good (elderly) folk of Walchurch gathered to play cards, buy subsidised drinks, swap gossip, and where overhead the theatre lay in complete darkness, with only the ghost of the lady in purple to walk the silent aisles.

"Must have been like Caerphilly Castle," commented Abby suddenly.

Des paused in mid sentence about the chill. "What must have been like Caerphilly Castle?"

"There." She gestured toward the centre. "The guide on that walk, when we first met, said Danverson Castle was standing right where the theatre is now. In that case, the village must have grown up around the castle gate, much as Caerphilly Castle is now. And Skenfrith."

"I missed that bit."

"I'm interested in the Danversons, which is why I went on the walk, why I'm going to the classes."

"Danverson. They've a chapel of their own in the church, haven't they?"

"Yes." Abby opened her front door with a practised swoop of the key, despite the dark. "Unfortunately I can't get in there, remember? It was all shut off for maintenance."

"That's right. Plenty of time for that."

Abby let him in, went swiftly to the bedroom and collected up some magazines. No sense in wasting time. Whatever he thought.

"Here." She pushed the magazines into his hands as he sat on the sofa, looking completely at home. "Have a quick look at the pictures, take them home to read the stories. I'll make some coffee. Or tea. Would you prefer tea?"

"Tea would be better."

"Sugar and milk in tea?"

"No sugar, thanks."

The arms were as thick as mooring posts, hands as rough as tarmac; they could hurt, they could be dangerous, they could be painful, they could be wonderful. Abby moved round her tiny kitchen area with practised ease, watching the kettle, setting out the mugs, spooning sugar into hers (forget the calories), pouring milk, thinking thoughts.

What was so special about the second time I went back to the inn for Des 'Mark I' to thrash me?

The anticipation.

I knew what I was going for.

I had time to think about it, to plan for it. As I sat here stitching a white skirt back into a condition sufficient to take me back, I knew what I was going for.

Anticipation.

Fear.

Oh yes, definitely fear. But fear of the most pleasurable kind.

What made Lord Danverson special, different from all the others? She paused, hand on the counter, wondering. Of all her travels to the past, the ones to

Danverson Castle had been different. The first and second times she had gone there it had been for the atmosphere, for the thrill of moving among elegant and beautiful people. She hadn't approached anyone until the third visit when Lord Danverson approached her. And that alone made those visits different, for on every other occasion she had found someone, got satisfaction and come back. Anticipation. Was that the key?

But I didn't know he was going to hurt me.

Oh no? What did the Mrs Dawson-Page lookalike warn you of?

Yes, but -

I knew nothing then of pain and pleasure, of s/m and all that it implied.

But you knew it was likely to be rough.

And you went. You obeyed his order, and you waited with wet pussy and aching need.

You obeyed.

There is something in you that recognised the masterful man even then, without prior knowledge.

The tea brewed. Abby picked up the tray and took it into the lounge where Des sat, surrounded by magazines.

"I'm only looking at the picture stories for now."

"Of course, you don't have time to read it all. Read a few readers' letters, though?"

"A few." He looked seriously at her. "This is important to you, isn't it?" He waved at the magazines. "You'd not invest this money if it wasn't."

"It's become important. It wasn't, not at first, but ... I've recognised a need in me, and I have to do something about it."

"What do you do about it?"

She handed him a mug and took her own, searching for a few seconds' thought. It was a question she hadn't anticipated. She lied but it was only half a lie.

"I have a master, someone I can go to."

"Would you tell me who it is?"

She grinned. "You wouldn't expect me to tell you, would you?"

"Can I learn to be a master?"

"Possibly, but it's something that comes instinctively. But you could learn to pleasure me."

"Give me a chance, Abby."

"Why is it so important to you?" She spoke lightly but feared the answer.

"I - I think you're something special. I don't want you to dump me just because I can't give you what you want." Good enough for now.

"Drink your tea." She gathered up the magazines, stacked them neatly on the coffee table. "The girls at work call me Sister Abigail; they believe I live a pure and chaste life. If they knew what we were discussing now, that you were here, that you'd been reading magazines ..."

He laughed, and put the mug down, empty.

"Come here." His voice was thick with lust, knowing in advance what would happen after. Even if it was all new for him, he was eager to try it all.

Abby stood up and walked over to the sofa, responding with her usual surge of anticipation/ sex/ fear/ need. "I'm ... bruised," she said softly. He shook his head.

"No matter. Over here." He gestured towards his legs, and she obediently lay down over him, toes just touching the floor, the usual fear churning away at her stomach, coupled with the thrills that reached all parts of her.

"Like this, isn't it?" He pulled up her skirt and yanked her knickers down hard, so that they formed a thin twisted line of material at mid-thigh. Abby felt the gusset bid a reluctant farewell to the wet and sticky slit of her pussy. Then he slapped hard at her cheek and she gasped.

Harder than she'd thought.

"Like that," she agreed, anticipating a firm spanking. His hand was as rough as tarmac, and it did hurt, a lot. Certainly more than if she hadn't had bruises. Before he had her bottom covered with red blotches she was squirming and fighting (but not too hard for fear of putting him off), feeling the familiar sensations of pain and heat, of wanting it to be over, yet longing for it to continue, thrilled at being made to take the punishment, knowing she needed it. She also registered his amateur efforts. After the firm expert spanking given to her by Sir Anthony, this was erratic, indiscriminate, not covering her as he should; but he could and would learn; It was, after all, a solid spanking and he acted as if he meant it.

Finally he let her slide to the floor, where she lay, red faced, running her hands through her hair, looking up at him, wondering how he had felt.

He looked puzzled.

"Abby, it felt ... right."

"So will this." She held out her arms and he slid to the floor, stripping off her panties, letting his fingers find her wet dripping slit, knowing she had loved it.

It was good, very good. Abby lay there, letting the waves of feeling sweep through her, half her mind loving every moment of it, the other half wondering how much had come through from the past. For someone not used to S/M he had done well, spanked hard, and - said it felt right.

There could be possibilities here, she thought, clinging to him and then giving up all thoughts of trying to everything in the waves of orgasm that hit her as he ground his hard length into her, rubbing against her clitoris but best of all digging his fingernails hard into her seared bottom as he rode her mercilessly.

Chapter 19: Now

"The castle, which was then known as Walchurch Castle, was started around 925, as far as we can tell." Sheila put up another of the endless slides on the screen. Abby cast a sharp glance at Des, who was taking notice of the lecture, not of her, for the first time that evening. "At that time the village would have been stone-and-timber houses, built around the castle for protection. The lord of the manor at that time was a Stewart, as far as we can tell. He started the castle building, which went on for over twenty years. Then there is a long period of comparative quiet and peace for the village. The timber wall around the church came down - the one which gave the village its name, incidentally - and the roads were improved so trade could carry on.

"A Danverson apparently went to war in the Crusades, and came home victorious. It was the custom at that time for monarchs to reward those who pleased them with land and buildings. The castle was empty, the Stewarts not having come back from the Crusades, so he was given the castle and grounds. There were Stewarts around but if any had a good claim to the castle, it didn't work, and anyway you didn't argue with the king. Danverson renamed it Castle Danverson, built even higher defences for it and added towers and courtyards. Danversons ruled the village and the area from their castle for close on 600 years."

Abby heard little more. For some reason, when anyone mentioned Danverson or she thought about it, all other thoughts disappeared, escaped from her mind.

I wish I could go back again, she told herself, but ...

Wishing wasn't enough. Something was holding her back from 'borrowing' the red-and-black or even the purple dress and going back to that time, to attending yet another ball at the castle. She felt she knew the castle. When she slipped back there to reclaim her dress, it had been like...

Coming home.

Trade and merchants, local dignitaries whose names she recognised all dated from that time, from the Crusades onward. Old families, well established, with roots deep enough to reach Australia. What had happened to the Danversons? Why hadn't they survived?

And the Stewarts? There had been Stewarts here who once owned the castle. Jefferson Nathaniel Stewart? Mrs Dawson-Page would have liked that bit.

"Coming, Abby?" She jerked herself back to the present, accepted Des' helping hand to get through the cluster of chairs pushed every which way by the departing class, and went out into the cold dark night.

Soft rain fell, coating the roofs and pavements with a lacquered shine. Cars cried tears, swept them away with a blink of windscreen eyelashes, went on crying as they dashed for home.

"Interesting stuff tonight." Des held a huge golf umbrella over her as they splashed through the puddles towards her flat. Without speaking about it, Abby knew that was where they were going.

"Yes, lots to think about."

"Think about? I don't think so!"

"Well -" Hastily flustering to cover her own thoughts, she said: "You know what I mean, names and families from around here to look for when we next go shopping."

"Oh yes, that kind of thinking about, of course."

"It seems some people's roots go deep around here."

"They sure do. Does your family have contacts here?"

"I didn't think so until this morning."

When the letter had arrived. Cousin Stephen, doing

107

some family research, looking for birth date and middle name confirmation, and telling her how far he had gone.

Almost to 1750. And a definite connection with the Danverson family. Could it be that they were linked in some way, which is why she had found it so easy to slip back to Danverson Castle, never having any problems?

"Abigail is a family name," he wrote. "There's been quite a few and certainly one or two in the Danverson family, so if you could let me know what middle name you have and confirm some dates, I'll see how it fits into the chart, and then let you have a copy later on."

She had written back during her lunch hour, confirming the dates and giving him her middle name, Guinevere, a name unusual enough to be an embarrassment to her, but one which might help him track the family back, as her mother had told her it was an old family name.

None of this she mentioned to Des; some things were best kept to herself.

To keep him happy she said lightly: "A family member is doing some research. We've been around here a long time, it seems." He seemed satisfied with that.

Back in the flat he looked at her with bright-eyed eagerness. "I'd like to repeat what we did the other night."

"I'm sure you would," she replied, with a teasing smile, feeling her stomach flip with pleasure. "Before or after I make some tea?"

"After. Give you time to think about it. I plan to use a slipper this time, Abby."

He's learning fast, thought Abby, going to the kitchen. Very fast. The old Des, the one in the past, is exerting considerable influence down the ages!

But hold on, not quite fast enough for our Des there; if he'd been a true dominant, and I'd sparked it from him, he wouldn't have asked, he'd have told me. And there would be no question that I would have to obey.

Which brings me back to Lord Danverson again.

Damn, each time someone wants to hurt me, I think of him!

Tea and small talk occupied half an hour, both of them skirting around the subject, Abby letting her slipper fall from her feet as if by accident, him picking one up as if to study it, then slipping it down the side of the cushion. Both knew what they were doing; neither said a word. It was a game, a sensual charade of silence and intimations.

Abby started a mock fight, pretending to scratch and pull Des' hair, he in turn pretended to struggle with her, both knowing what would happen. With a tug she ended up over his knees again, staring at the floor, wishing desperately for someone who knew what they were doing, berating herself for being unfair to Des, when the slipper landed on an exposed cheek and stung more than she thought it would.

"That's different." Des spanked the other cheek. "No pressure on the old hands, no stinging palm, only stinging you!"

Writhing over Des' knee as he brought the rubber-soled slipper down with devastating force, Abby began to revise her opinion. It might just be possible for someone to learn to be a dominant after all.

CHAPTER 20: THEN

Sunshine, the smell of resin, sawdust and oil, of farmland and all things growing. Abigail glanced down at a strange outfit she had cobbled together: high boots, trousers, a sort of smock and large floppy brimmed hat. She had aimed for, and succeeded, it seemed, in going back further than the World War II land girl scenario, and gone for the earlier women's Land Army of the First World War.

Just to see what it was like.

The clothes felt coarse and uncomfortable. She wondered how anyone could work in such an outfit.

"Hey, you!" The voice was hard, and female. "What are you slacking for? Get on with it!"

"Sorry." Abigail moved towards a large shed, wondering what it was she was supposed to be doing. The woman, stern faced, grey-red hair, charged after her.

"I don't recognise you, do I? Where did you come from?"

"I've been ... sent here," she said in truth,

"Well? Who sent you? Come on, I don't need any more of you females around distracting my men!"

"Might not be here long," Abigail floundered madly.

"Well, good, for all the use you are! Get in that shed and start stacking logs! Now!"

Abigail hurried towards the shed, her boots clumsy on her feet.

The shed was dark, loaded with dirt, grime and crawling things. She disturbed a nest of woodlice and jumped back, repulsed by the creeping armoured bodies.

"Scared of a few crawlies? Damn townies, they're all alike." A male voice this time. Abigail spun around to see a weathered man looking at her. Ageless, with a face so lined and hard he could have been any age from thirty to sixty.

"They give me the creeps." Abigail dusted her hand down her smock, wondering if this was the person she'd come to see. Could he read the 'I'm available' sign stamped on her forehead?

He moved closer - then possibly he could.

"You ain't from around here."

"No, I'm not."

"No, I mean you ain't one of the land girls I been seeing for some time."

"No, I'm not," she repeated, feeling foolish.

"Come." He gestured towards a little cottage set on the edge of the woods. Abigail obediently followed, wondering what she would find; the mirror was always on her mind, finding it, getting back to Real Time.

The cottage was damp, masculine and drab. No pictures ornamented the stained old walls, the plaster was bowing and threatening to fall at any time. A fire was laid but remained unlit, the table and chairs were scarred and battered. He saw her looking, and sighed.

"Missus over there don't think much of the workers on the farm. We get what they don't want."

Abigail followed him into the bedroom, wondering just how big the 'I'm available' sign really was that any man could see it so clearly, or ...

When she went back to a particular point, in a particular place, was the man she met expecting a session with a woman? It was a question to be pondered later, when the fucking was done.

"You be a fair one and no mistake. No dirt under the nails, no dirt in the skin. My, how white you are." Her clothes came off, one at a time. She had a bad moment with the lace bra, but he didn't seem to notice. And it didn't matter. Shivering with cold and damp, she allowed herself to be touched, her nipples sucked and nibbled, the feelings swamping her as always. It didn't seem to matter that the man was of indeterminate age and certainly dirty with farm soil and probably animals; it didn't matter if the fingers were finding all the nerve ends, making her jump, making her squeal with pleasure.

"My, you be a fine one and no mistake." No wasting time, either - no doubt time on the farm was precious. Missus wouldn't like them taking half an hour to do what could be done in ten minutes. His cock hard and sure, they fell back on a lumpy mattress and made the bed shake as he entered her, hot and wet and ready, desperate for the feel of it all, desperate for an extra inch, an extra half inch, looking for depth and finding it. Large balls crushed against her pubis, pleasuring her more. She pulled him closer, held his buttocks, attempted to keep him hard against her.

When the first rush of passion was over, Abigail looked at him with calculating eyes. She reached for the still-stiff cock, played with it, felt it stiffen even more and smiled.

"My turn." She rolled him over onto his back, mounted him, feeling him go even harder as he slid into her. She pressed her knees hard against his sides. He stroked her naked pubis and smiled.

"Don't see too many of them around here. How'd you do it?" She didn't answer. He rubbed her nipples with a circular movement, caressed her breasts, opened his mouth in a silent scream as she rode him to her second shattering orgasm.

"My, I ain't ever had one like that!" he told her as she eased herself off him and lay panting and lethargic, on his cold lumpy bed. "You be one rare fine woman."

"Find me a drink." She traced his chest hair with a sensual finger.

"Of course, anything for a fine white lady." He slipped

on old baggy underpants and left the bedroom, muttering 'slut' under his breath as he left. Abigail knew that was his real opinion of her.

As soon as he had gone Abby snatched up her ugly clothes and looked in the mirror.

Stewarts. She hadn't noticed that before when they were on the tour. They were all Stewarts: died in India, in South Africa during the Boer War, and earlier, of smallpox and childbirth. Stewarts everywhere.

And Danversons?

The moment could not be delayed much longer. The Danverson Chapel was almost - almost - clear to view.

A huge monument on the wall gave mute testimony to a Danverson - Thomas James - Rear Admiral, man of God, father of 10 children, who lived his life in the service of God and of this country, died at sea August 1648, and was mourned by his loving wife and all his children.

A kneeling monument, life-size, of a beautiful serene lady with hands in the classic position for prayer. A board hanging by a piece of string on the wall told Abby that this was Margaret Elizabeth, wife of Josiah Thomas Danverson, much loved, died in childbirth in 1616.

Which meant that the table tomb had to be the man himself.

Josiah Thomas Danverson. Yes, it suited the man with the Van Dyck beard, the piercing eyes and dominant manner, the one who so obviously ruled his household with a rod of iron. Had he loved Margaret Elizabeth a lot? And were there any children living from the marriage? Was Thomas James Danverson the son of Margaret Elizabeth and Josiah Thomas?

The tomb was still covered with heavy tarpaulin, weighed down with stones and iron bars, but she could surely lift the side of it, gently, just the side, to try and read more of the man who was haunting her every thought and most of her dreams.

JOSIAH THOMAS DANVERSON
6th June 1591 - 17th May 1673
For Glory and For Love

Abby stared at the words, tracing them with her fingers, not believing what she was reading.

The name of the play she was in was carved here in ancient beautiful script: For Glory and for Love.

What kind of epitaph was that?

She tried to walk around the tomb, but there were chairs stacked twelve high at the back, blocking her way. She tried to lift the tarpaulin even further but couldn't because of the bricks and bars.

"I wouldn't disrupt the work." A soft voice. She spun round in surprise. The vicar smiled at her.

"Just visiting? I don't recognise you."

"Just visiting." She smiled tremulously, feeling her heart pounding from the shock. "I had a letter the other day from a relative who is researching family history. He said we were possibly related to the Danversons, so I came to have a look at the tomb."

"The roof leaked badly up there." He pointed to the water stained walls. "We've had this cordoned off for ages, but they're getting there now. The tomb will be revealed soon. Can I help with any further information?"

"Well..." Abby rubbed at her forehead. "I want to know all sorts of things, like ... is Thomas James Danverson the son of Josiah and Margaret? I saw the monument - " she pointed to the wall and then the kneeling figure. "And did Lord Danverson marry again and -"

"Let's look in the records, see what we can find. I'm not sure how much the Historical Society found out, but we might be able to find something."

The vestry was a tiny cramped room with clerical cloaks hanging from ancient hooks on the ancient door, a worn pump handle to one side of a huge safe that would have kept a safe cracker out for all of five minutes, a huge framed map of the graveyard done by the local Historical Society, boxes and tables and registers.

The vicar was everyone's idea of a vicar, small, white-haired with glasses, and a calming soothing voice, almost the stereotypical parson. Did the profession make the man or the man enter the profession because he looked the part? Foolish thoughts.

"We do have something about the Danversons here, but not a lot." He turned over typewritten sheets. "It seems Josiah Danverson married Margaret Stewart and they had three children, Thomas James, Henrietta Margaret and Edward. She died giving birth to Edward and he died shortly after. The records indicate that later Lord Danverson married again, an Abigail Brandon, apparently, and they went on to have several children, some of whom died. Here are the notes-"

The vestry was reeling. Literally. Solid stone walls flashed by, the world went around, and Abby clung to the table.

"Are you all right, my dear? You look as if you've had a terrible shock. Can I get you anything?"

"No, I'll be all right in a minute. I just came over a bit faint, that's all."

"Well, if you're sure -" he didn't look very sure, but turned back to the notes. "There's mention of a son, Josiah, named for his father, no doubt, a daughter, Guinevere, another son David. I think the Historical Society could help you further but that's what we have here."

"Thank you, you've been most helpful, I think I'll get some fresh air. Thank you very much."

"Come again, the tomb will be uncovered before too long."

"Thanks, I will." Abbey clicked rapidly through the crowd of pews, feeling as if every one had someone sitting in them, someone who stared with large eyes, stared so hard they made holes in her clothes, melting …

The air was cool and fresh after the rain, there was a smell of grass and leaves, birds calling, the graves sleeping under their moisture-laden blankets.

All right, so he married an Abigail Brandon. So, we are linked to the Danversons. I wonder why the Brandons stayed around and the Danversons didn't? Perhaps the line died out, perhaps later there were only girls. Makes sense. But -

My name.

As if -

As if it were me back then, married to Josiah Danverson, giving birth to his children, in that time.

Which means -

She shook her head, unable to comprehend the enormity of the thoughts.

I can't cope with this.

I'm going home.

To seek refuge in my book.

CHAPTER 22: NOW

The mirror is strange, and unpredictable. It has occurred to me that it probably didn't have these magical powers in the past, or superstitious people would have smashed it long ago, so when did it start giving people access to the past? And how? And who first noticed it? Did they go and never come back?

And what happened to the theory that the time which passes while you are in the past is the same as the time which passes in the present, which means I should come back several hours later than I leave, but I don't.

Different time-travel methods have different time-travel effects.

My theory for the day.

Such things can never be answered, for there is no one to answer them.

But it is strange and unpredictable.

A 1910 outfit borrowed from the theatre, hobble skirt, long-line jacket, hat with feathers, sent me back to a dark and gloomy pub somewhere I did not recognise. Sawdust floor, scarred bar top, tables and chairs the worse for wear, smoke-dulled ceiling, beer-stained walls. A most unsavoury place. In another time and another place I'd have left and demanded my companion take me somewhere more salubrious.

But here - well, it didn't matter.

The barman, a large man with a broken face, looked like an ex-boxer and probably was. It occurred to me also that I'd never seen a small man tending bar; a small man would have to be a karate expert of some kind to control unruly customers and eject drunks, so on the whole they tended to be large men with strong arms and shoulders. There's also the heaving of the ale barrels around and a million other things. I wanted a strong man.

One who came with arms and shoulders of steel, one who would give me what I wanted - a long hard ride.

Damn the feelings which drive me to this!

No, love the feelings which drive me to this.

An unaccompanied woman, a magnet for all eyes and all men.

In about three seconds flat I was accosted by a man at the bar: tall, thin, blackened teeth, soiled skin, someone who works with coal? Or industrial waste of some kind? There was a smell around his clothes, not quite coal, not quite chemicals, somewhere in between. I could not place it.

"A drink." It wasn't a request, and that suited me.

"Rum and lime." My standard drink for the past. A safe drink, small, easy to dispose of, for I was careful (then) not to touch anything, to make sure I brought nothing back with me, other than come, which only allowed some woman somewhere a few months' freedom from childbearing; there was more where that came from.

We talked over drinks. I pretended to drink, and poured some away when no one was looking; very very occasionally, for even with a companion all eyes were on me all of the time. But I tipped a little into the ashtray, into the spittoon at the side of me, and managed to spill some accidentally too.

A roll of notes appeared in my hand as if by magic, a thick roll, solid banknotes, the like of which I had not seen before.

"Take what you want from there, girlie. Take what you want and come in my van with me."

"Let's go and look at the van first," I suggested, seeing his eyes light up; before they had held hope, now they held certainty and lust.

A sigh went round the men as we left, me with an unfinished drink on the table, another man made for it as we reached the door. A sigh that was for the man who had snared me first and for the lost chances, for they could have and should have been two seconds faster than he was.

I would have gone with any of them.

The van was parked outside, lonely, proud, shining with newness and money.

I got inside, marvelling at the Spartan layout, the crude wiper blades, the clang of the door as it shut. My companion (I never knew his name) proudly crank-started it with the large starting handle, leapt in and we were away, driving out of Walchurch, an old Walchurch I did not recognise at first.

"Unusual to see a lady alone in the old Compasses, my dear."

Compasses. I remembered the pub from old photographs. It burned down in 1950-something.

"There are times when only a direct approach will do," I said, laughing.

He laughed too. "I know what you means, which is why I handed you the cash, my dear. You can take what you want, take it all, if you want. I haven't had anyone for ... "

I wasn't surprised, with breath like that and so drink-sodden that no woman of normal needs would go with you.

I said nothing, but waited until we drew up in a side lane in the woods outside Walchurch, woods that were thicker and more extensive than now.

We climbed in the back, and on a blanket or two, with nuts and the spare wheel occasionally hitting our bodies, we rocked the van for half an hour: him hard and fast and furious, me desperate and seeking every half inch, every thrust, every emotion sweeping through me.

But even I, at the end of half an hour, had taken enough of the smell of ale and the teeth which were coated and foul.

I said I was sore. He said thanks, it was wonderful, best he'd had in his life, ever, and I pushed the money back at him.

"Just take me back to the pub," I said, "I need no money to make love."

"You be the first ever." He grinned, even more pleased as he stowed his wad of cash back into his filthy coat.

The men in the pub were so surprised, you could see their eyes as I walked through the door, the man with the van holding my arm, and asked where the ladies' toilet was.

"Don't have such a thing," said the barman, "but you can go upstairs into my quarters if you like."

And I did and the mirror was waiting and I fled...

"How's the boyfriend, Ab?" Linda paused on her way out the door, eager for gossip. Abby had been so busy, snowed under with heaps of files and tapes all stacked up on the door, she'd hardly had a moment to talk to her fellow work slaves.

"Fine, very nice, we're still going out."

"Seeing him tonight, are you?"

"No, we have a full dress rehearsal tonight for the play."

"Oh, getting close to the night then."

"Only a week away."

"Have a good time. Hope it goes well, oops, sorry, break a leg." Linda disappeared, leaving Abby to finish the file she was dealing with, close down her machine and cover everything up for the night.

Des was all right, very keen, very anxious to make an impression in every sense of the word! But there was still something missing, something not quite right. I think he's trying too hard, she thought, as she slipped on her coat and hurried down the stairs.

"Good night, Mr Brooks." She smiled at him as she went quietly out.

"Night, Abby." Miles away, as usual, deep in a law book.

It was getting dark; the street lights sending down their orange light that drained colour out of everything. Cars flashed by in a swirl of light and red and were gone, traffic lights changed with the monotony of the night stars, slow, dogged, never-ending. Shops invited her in but she resisted, hurrying homeward. Cats dropped like liquid fur onto the pavement, eyes flashing like traffic lights and were gone, a clatter of dustbin lids, the yap of a dog, the sound of feet passed her.

"Goodnight." Someone passing by, acknowledging the existence of another human being, faceless in the gloom.

There was time - just - for a quick meal and then off to the theatre for a full dress rehearsal, with sets and backdrops and everything, she hoped.

'For Glory and for Love.'

Coincidence.

Of course.

Like his marrying an Abigail Brandon, like their having a daughter Guinevere.

Like the feeling of wanting to go home, except that home wasn't this poky little flat with a door which stuck in the damp but a huge draughty castle with tapestries and stone stairs with fine carved wooden objects and handmade furniture, with dogs which welcomed her (how did they know?) and a page who thought she was a ghost. Why else did he run so fast?

"Come on," she told herself. "No time for all that, there are things to be done!"

But the thoughts persisted, even as she ate a swift microwave meal, snapping the radio off in annoyance. Lately the music had begun to irritate and annoy her, no matter what it was. She had tried Radio 3 and Classic FM, but even the lilting strains of the more gentle composers clashed and grated on her ears. She changed clothes for the evening, an easy slip on dress so she could slip into what felt best - the purple dress with its huge lace collar and full skirt.

The theatre was half-dark when Abby arrived, carrying the purple dress and button boots, her hair already pinned up ready to disappear under the cap. She hurried to change, and then took a long walk round the building, trying to find the places which had been built from or on top of the original castle walls. With modern plastering and possibly plasterboard in position, it was hard to find the exact spots, so she gave up looking and went by touch instead.

Here and there coolness reached out to her; here, this whole wall was surely once castle. Or was castle stones. It spoke to her of misty twilights, of the sadness of autumn, of the chequerboard fields she could see from narrow leaded windows. It filled her with the strangest homesickness she had ever felt.

The long corridor from the dressing rooms to the stage: cold and damp, here and here...

"Oh, my God! You're doing it again!" Abby spun round at the cry and ran to Jim Melville's side. He had gone white, hands shaking, leaning against the wall.

"Sorry, Mr Melville, I was ... just walking along." She blushed, hoping he wouldn't notice.

"You were just like that lady in purple, floating along there, following the old castle walls, they do say."

Abby stiffened. It was the first time she had heard such a tale.

"Is that the legend, Mr Melville?"

"It is." He gulped a few times, massaged his heart, stared at her in the semi-darkness. "They say the lady comes along here, along the castle wall, goes up the stairs and disappears."

Of course she does. I went to the mirror and never came back.

"I'm so sorry. I never meant to frighten you like that."

"It's all right. I oughta get used to you people dressed like that while this damn play's going on!"

"Bit too close to the ghost, is it?' she asked almost playfully.

"Damn right. Even the name of the play gives me the shivers. Wish I knew what was going on around here." He pushed himself off the wall and went on down the corridor. "Stay on the stage, Goodwife Manderson!"

Abby went cold all over.

When Alfred said it he used his upper class accent, and made it sound ... trivial.

Jim Melville said it with a more colloquial sound, and it could have been Danverson.

Manderson.

Danverson.

Who wrote this play, anyway?

Even the name of the play gives me the shivers.

It hadn't affected her until she had visited the church and seen Josiah's tomb.

I don't understand.

I don't understand anything that is going on, I just feel... I am in the wrong place at the wrong time.

So, I will go and be Goodwife Manderson for an hour or so, until the charade is over.

Until I find a way of becoming Goodwife Danverson forever,

She wondered where that thought came from.

CHAPTER 24: NOW

The Georgian lord was fun.

A bit of a dandy, with powdered wig and silk breeches, ribbons and orange water, he talked in an affected voice but had the stamina of a stallion. The mirror sent me back to his grounds where I walked in solitary splendour, my skirts long and elegant, whispering around me as I strolled beside his lake. He soon saw me, that 'I'm available for sex' sign flashing like neon through the summer afternoon. He crossed the lawn in huge strides, his coat flying free, his wig threatening to become a casualty of speed.

"Madam." He bowed and I curtsied - I'm getting good at that.

"Welcome." No questions asked. Another oddity; no one really asks, no one says 'How did you get here, why you here, why aren't I having you thrown out?' they accept. Mirror magic, of course.

"Could I persuade you to take some refreshment?"

"That would be most kind." We walked into the huge house, hall and rooms hung with expensive oil paintings that would fetch a fortune today, sombre ancestors glared down from flocked walls and gilt frames.

Servants scurried to his command, eyeing me strangely but saying nothing; well-trained, they were. Tea was brought in delicate cups you could almost see through. I was almost scared to touch them.

I think the sign must have been flashing, for no sooner had he drunk his tea and I had scarcely touched my lips to mine than he suggested a game.

Of hide-and-seek.

Of all things!

So we played hide-and-seek around this huge house, with many rooms and galleries, with staircases and closets, kissing and touching and struggling with one another until we finally ended up in his bedroom, windows hung wide to the cool fast-approaching evening. Somewhere across the fields came the wail of a huntsman's horn; nearer, the scent of lilac drifted in to coat the air with sweetness and sensuality.

We stopped hunting and he found me and we fucked for ages. One of the best, my Georgian lord, one of the best.

Until I went to Castle Danverson. Danverson Castle.

Whatever and whichever.

Castle Danverson.

My first visit was in midwinter, snow thick everywhere, deep and obscuring, the view from the windows distorted by the blanket of white, by snow piled on narrow sills. It looked magnificent, trees holding up their snowy branches, fields pristine white, no tracks, no tractors, no mud.

From every sconce hung mistletoe and holly, ivy wound around the shields and pikes which decorated the walls, a huge log burning with vicious strength, sending sparks of blue green and purple into the hearth. The scent of green growing things, of sap and fertility. Midwinter feast, Christmas in all but name. I mingled with the guests, many of them wearing heavy clothes, for even with the Yule log the castle was cold. They drank mulled wine and mead, toasted His Lordship and mentioned in passing his great loss, and how he was coping with it. I mingled and spied on His Lordship, caught him looking at me but stayed well out of his way. Made friends with his dogs, petting them, getting huge adoring eyes and paws on my dress, but they were fine animals, and soon responded to a loving touch and a soft voice. It was the first time I had gone back to the past and not found a man.

I knew who I wanted, but I was afraid of him, afraid of approaching him, afraid of what he might say if he found out who I was.

I was simply afraid.

For the first time ever.

I found no man to fuck with, despite many casual invitations and hands resting on arms, a look that could not be ignored. I turned them all down, wanting only one man, and not having the courage to approach him.

I finally slipped away and found the mirror in a drawing room, framed by tapestries, and sent myself home. Frustrated and lonely.

How did the mirror know to send me back to a midsummer ball next time? I went back a week later - in his life, six months later - and saw him again, the small beard glistening in the sunlight filtering through the leaded windows, carrying with it the scents of summer, apple and grass, rich-growing land and vibrant herds, horses galloping for the sheer love of it, rolled in the thick grass in their paddock. Birds hunted and sang, animals prowled the perimeters of my Lord's land.

Guests were happy and smiling, enjoying the celebrations. Ladies wore Saint John's Wort corsages, and the dogs jumped around me as I walked near the great hearth. I felt at home and yet I lacked the confidence or the courage to approach the one man who attracted me.

Oh, he looked, time and again he looked, casual, off-hand, but he never approached me and never so much as a word passed between us.

I went to the drawing room very soon and disappeared out of his life.

I thought forever.

And then Alfred Fitzpaine came to the theatre with a script in his hand, written by a local historian, he said, called 'For Glory And For Love' and the words tingled down my spine and I knew I wanted to be in it. I knew it had something to say to me if not to the audience who would come.

We voted to do the play and he accorded me instantly the role of Goodwife Manderson.

I could relate here and now the words, the role, the part I play, but it is small, relatively insignificant, for Stevie and Charles have the main roles, Stevie and Charles play the roles ... well, Stevie plays the role ... say it!

I would play if I were Lady Danverson.

And it took me until today to realise that my part, my character, is close to Danverson in sound and spelling.

Where have I been all this time not to see it and feel it before?

And the ghost.

Oh yes, the ghost.

Poor Jim Melville.

This is no longer a book, is it? If it ever was. It's a commentary, a record in case I never come back. So let me put it all down.

I went to a midsummer ball at Castle Danverson, wearing red and black and a lot of courage.

Lord Danverson approached me; we talked, I knew this time I could not and would not give way to my cowardice, so I went to his room and waited.

And he came. I stripped off the red-and-black dress, threw it to one side and ... we made love. And I know this is the first time I've written that in this entire commentary so far, but with him it was not simple fucking, with him it went deeper than that; he touched a deeper chord in me.

We made love for some time, good love. He was hard and firm and good and knew how to pleasure me. He made me cry out with pleasure, he made me claw at the bedhead and coarse linen sheets with pure joy for the feelings wrought in me with his thrusting cock and his fingers, his tongue and his whole lean body. The beard tickled in secret places, the muscles rippled and moved under my fingers and it was good.

And I know I pleased him. Yet he pulled me off the bed, bound my wrists with a girdle from his robe, and sent his page, the same one who had directed me to his room in the first place, to get a birch.

Which confused me.

I knew nothing of such things. I knew nothing of pain and pleasure. I knew nothing of a birch which was a bundle of whippy twigs tied together on a handle and which he used with devastating force on my bottom, my thighs and my back. I broke free of my restraints, I looked in the mirror and -

Came back here, naked and sore.

It was only when I went to the next rehearsal and Alfred mentioned Stevie wearing the red and black that I realised I'd left something of critical value in the past, something out of its time, with machine stitching, and machine-made lace. I had to get it back.

I donned the purple dress, my replacement costume for the play and went back into the past, back to Castle Danverson, to recover the dress.

I went at night, when the dogs were sleeping, when the brindle bitch, my favourite, woke from rabbit-chasing dreams to see me then went back to sleep, and I went up the stairs along the corridor to Lord Danverson's room. The page was sleeping on the floor at the door. He woke, saw me and fled in what looked like sheer terror.

I entered Lord Danverson's room and of course never appeared again.

To the page I must have seemed like a ghost.

To me it was just common sense to go back and recover the dress, so I wouldn't have explanations to give to Alfred, not that he would ever know it was me who lost it.

I have just had a single illuminating flash of thought.

The servant who handed my Lord Danverson his tankard of ale is the living image, the very double, the identical twin, of Kenneth Thompson.

How did I feel, sore and naked and birched? How did I feel? Confused. Hurt. Mixed up. It was the first time I had come back hurt: it was the first time I had come back crying.

The next morning, long before I thought of having to return, I had a new feeling to contend with.

Satisfaction.

Chapter 25: Now

Unlike most evening classes, the local history talks had remained well attended. There was not an empty chair in Sheila Grantham's front room.

"We know where most of the original castle stood." A sketch plan flashed onto the screen. "See where the dotted outlines are? That's where the original foundations of the castle were. You'll see in places it is much larger than the King's Theatre which was built on the site."

"Does anyone know why the land stood empty for a hundred years?" asked Abby, leaning forward for a better look at the sketch plan. I walked most of that, she told herself. I'll find the rest, get round the back of the theatre, where they store all that old rubbish, walk the rest. The castle's bigger than I realised, but then, I've yet to find the kitchens and the stables, and other outhouses.

"Superstition." Sheila Grantham grinned, her face bone-white in the light from the projector. "The story of the lady in purple persisted for ages! And then there was the Walchurch Curse, or as it became known, the Danverson Curse. Anyone who tried to build something there, who moved the stones, or dug foundations, got hurt in some way. When two or three people were killed, they gave up."

"What do we know about the ghost?" asked someone else. Abby heaved a small sigh of relief; she didn't want it to be her making the running all the time. Des squeezed her hand and smiled. He didn't know about the ghost and Jim Melville. She'd tell him later.

"We think she dates from the time of the castle itself, as she wears this flowing purple dress with lace collar, her hair up in a cap, very much a lady from the early 1600s. She walks around the walls, goes up the stairs and disappears."

"How often has she been seen?" Someone else.

"Quite a few times, apparently. Whoever she is, the story persisted that she was guarding the site, not letting anything be built on it. And as there was no pressing need to build on it and there were plenty of other sites in Walchurch, it was left alone."

"How come the theatre got built?" asked Des, involved in the story now. Even for disbelievers, it was a tale.

"This is the strangest part of the whole story." Another plan appeared on the screen, showing arrows this time. "We always get asked about the ghost, so we drew a rough indication of where she walks. The peculiar thing is, she, whoever she is, or the curse, if that's what it was, came into effect if someone tried to build a house or a shop or offices on the site. When a sign went up saying they were going to build a theatre, nothing happened. She, the curse, whatever, didn't mind a theatre being built, but refused to allow the other buildings. So, we have a theatre and Community Centre. And a fine one it is, too."

More slides of the theatre, black and white, as it changed its portico, as it modernised, to today.

Abby sat in complete silence, as if turned to stone.

I needed the theatre there.

I need the theatre there.

To get the costumes.

To go back.

"Incidentally the Danverson motto was 'For Glory and For Love'. I took that as the title for the play I wrote. It's being performed at the King's Theatre just next week, isn't that right, Miss Brandon?" Sheila Grantham again.

Abby blushed as everyone looked at her.

"Yes, that's right. I - I have a small part in it."

"I got the idea after researching the whole period of the 1600s and it seemed right to link it with local dignitaries."

"Sounds like it might be good." A voice from the other corner of the room.

Be fair, thought Abby, tell them now.

"I would just warn you, if you're coming to the play, that I wear a purple dress. I've already been mistaken twice for the ghost by the caretaker!"

A ripple of amusement ran round the room. Sheila snorted with delight.

"What a lovely story! I'll have to remember that for the next set of talks!"

Soon after that the class broke up for the evening. Des walked with Abby to the door.

"I'd like to stay with you for a while tonight but I think I'm coming down with a cold," he apologised, his eyes red and his nose already running. He snuffled into a handkerchief. "I don't want to give it to you."

"Walk to the door with me, then you're on your way home anyway." Abby tucked her arm through his, and they went out into the cold night.

They walked in silence, comfortable in each other's company, Des occasionally sneezing and coughing.

"You need to get home and into bed," Abby warned solicitously. "Go on with you, get some whisky and lemon down you or something!"

"I'll call you when I'm better."

"Do that."

He turned to go, but came back.

"I almost forgot this. I picked it up for you, not had a chance to look at it yet." A small book, locally printed: the history of Walchurch. "One of Sheila Grantham's efforts. Thought you might like to have a read." He sneezed violently. "Good-night, Abby."

"Night, Des. Go home, stay warm."

She watched him walk away along the road into the darkness, feeling suddenly lonely.

What a foolish thought! I've been alone ever since I left home! And with family relations the way they are, I'll go on being lonely!

Her flat wasn't welcoming any more, not since she had experienced other places, other walls, other people.

A castle.

She made herself tea, switched on her electric blanket, and curled up on the sofa with the little book. It was something to read before going to bed.

Much of what Abby read already been covered in the talks, the history of Walchurch, early sketches of how the church might have looked, an early sketch of the castle ...

That made her pause for a while. She had never seen the Castle from the outside, never appreciated the soaring towers, the slit windows, the huge moat with its heavy drawbridge and portcullis ready to drop. A solid place, impregnable, standing firm against foe and weather alike. Oh yes, that was a castle and just how it should look. It felt right. Whoever had put the picture together had a feel for the rightness of it.

A photograph of the Danverson tomb. Lord Josiah Thomas Danverson, flat on his back, hands clasped on his chest, his small beard in place, a dog at his feet. The stonemason had captured him in all his handsome glory. The family motto, 'For Glory and for Love', stood out clearly from the rich carving at the base of the tomb, with an heraldic shield alongside and flowing greenery surrounding it all.

She couldn't see the person lying alongside Lord Danverson, the other Abigail Brandon. That would have to wait until she could get back in the church and see it when the covers had been removed, when the Danverson Chapel was open to the public once again.

When the play is over, she told herself, I'll borrow the red-and-black dress and try to get back one more time to another of Lord Danverson's festivities, try to see some more of the castle, try to see how I feel when I'm there.

But for now, well, I might as well go write some more of my commentary. No Des, no sex, and tonight I'm not up to dressing up to go somewhere. I had just hoped ...

CHAPTER 26: NOW

A society lunch, very Edwardian, elegant ladies in dresses, ruffled parasols, jewellery glinting in the sun. The men so smart with cravats and stick-pins, sticks with silver-and-gold tops, polished boots, polished faces, well-fed paunches. So elegant, so smooth, so ... suffocatingly dull.

He was nice-looking, the man I picked from the lunch, the man who appeared to be alone and who, as it turned out was alone. He was wifeless, she being at home with the ague, the ladylike illness that could be anything from a period stomach-ache or a simple not wanting to go.

We soon left the lunch, since the 'I'm available' sign was flickering away like crazy, and he read it and we left.

His club was all dark panelling and serious members, eyes peering over glasses and from behind papers, rustling with righteous indignation and jealousy.

We departed for the upstairs room allocated to Sir Anthony.

He wasted no time at all, a quick hug, arms around and before I knew what was happening I was being spanked. Hard.

How could such a man, no doubt with servants to attend to his every need, from shoe polishing to gardening, hurt so much with a white soft hand?

But he did and it was an experience.

And then he sat on the side of the bed and played with me and fingered me, thrusting fingers and then most of his hand deep inside me, bringing me to orgasm. His cock never entered me. I gave him pleasure afterwards, but it wasn't the same.

I missed the solid cock ramming into me. Oh he was good, very expert, but Lady whatever-her-name-was no doubt had a bad sex life, for he was obviously impotent.

And he, for the first time, opened my eyes to the fact that men like to spank women just for the hell of it.

I knew then what Lord Danverson was about. And why the Mrs Dawson-Page lookalike so many years back told me he was a cruel man who liked to hurt women.

What I'd like to know is, how did she know?

The experience left me low. I needed a real experience, a real man. I donned my Dusty Springfield outfit and took off for the 1960s.

The City of London. Full of men in bowlers and women in smart designer clothes, high-heels and briefcases, moving alongside their contemporaries as if they owned the place, which for the most part they probably did. I bought a spanking magazine from a man at a news-stand in Fleet Street, endured his leer of pure lust, handed over a one pound note I had rescued from a coin dealer. I walked to Fenchurch Street, walked along the kerb but still could not avoid the men who so nonchalantly swung an arm and contacted with my pubis, brushed against a breast, half apologised and were gone before you could decide what the look had been saying.

The station was full of old memories of steam, dust, dirt and grime. Full of commuters all scurrying here, there and everywhere. Bought a coffee at a stall with money also rescued from the coin dealer. Read the magazine over coffee, which I did not then drink, still afraid of what might happen if I really did take something back, other than come.

Queued for the telephone in a line long enough to ensure I had something to do for some time; when I got three calls away from the telephone I muttered, looked at my watch and walked off. Not one eye blinked; everyone was doing the same, impatient, anxious.

Out of the station, back down the now-deserted road, jut the late workers hurrying home to wife, children and fireside to show any kind of life.

And I walked into a sleepy off-the-beaten-track courtyard in the City of London, earlier full of men in bowlers and suits but now, late, deserted, left to dust and golden glow from a gas lamp and gloomy with a big church. The inn was inviting. I had no choice but to go in. And I did and I met two men.

My instinct let me down.

The man behind the bar was dark, lowering, with thick arms and heavy eyebrows. He wore a belt strong enough to moor the Queen Elizabeth. He looked a bit dirty.

And, I fastidious even then, though why I didn't know, went for the smooth-talking elegantly groomed businessman.

Nigel. In a suit.

And a City flat. Where we fucked and rolled around in ecstasy. He knew how to fuck but ignored my need, shown by my unrolling the magazine onto the counter top.

So I went back to the inn, drawn back to the inn, for the mirror was not in Nigel's City flat.

And the barman knew what I had come back for. He touched his belt and indicated he knew how to deal with a woman the way she needed to be dealt with.

And I stayed, and I went to his room and he thrashed me harder than I'd been beaten by anyone, even by Lord Danverson. A belt hurts in the way a birch cannot and will not.

The leather bit and stung and hurt, drove me crazy. I couldn't wait for it to be over, but afterwards, oh, the afterwards, when he pulled me up on my hands and knees and rammed deep into me, so deep I thought he would burst me wide apart, and I knew then. This, yes, this was what I wanted.

Oh Des, if you ever read this, I wasn't being unfaithful to you, not really! For he looked just like you or you looked just like him, I can't decide which it is!

And I lied to Alfred and said I'd slipped and hurt my coccyx when I couldn't walk smoothly at rehearsal the next day.

I read my magazines in the safety of my flat, spent a fortune on them from the Private Shop, if only Sue and Linda knew how many times I'd crossed those forbidden portals and bought forbidden magazines! If only they knew what Sister Abigail got up to out of hours, when the mirror called and I obeyed the summons, and stepped in front of it...

To be whisked back to the past and into a different life.

Where all that mattered was sex and no worries about a reputation.

What more could anyone ask?

CHAPTER 27: NOW

Everyone agreed that the play was a stunning success. For three nights the King's Theatre was full, for three nights a story set in 1625 unfolded across the stage, bringing a touch of the past, a moment of glory and a story of love, to the audience.

Abby walked the boards, spoke her lines, stood in the wings and dreamed her dreams.

The applause was welcome, but more than that, the costume, the dialogue, the feel was right. More at home there than in her modern short clothes and office environment. More at home in this, the distant past, where life was much harder yet simpler, where simple pleasures became important, where financial considerations were not for women to worry about. For a while the unreal world of lights, wooden stage, wings, painted backdrop and props, was more real than her small flat, more real than the supermarket and the shops, more real than the cold dressing rooms and chilled corridors.

If I were there, she mused, watching Stevie pout through the play, dazzling under the lights, I'd be thinking the other way round. For my man would be important to me, more important than anything else, so the motto would be 'For Love and for Glory'. And I'd give a great deal to have a man to love to the exclusion of all else.

Des? He's nice, he's all right, but he isn't The One. He doesn't stir me deep inside. It's not a problem to me not to see him for these three nights, not a problem to send him home at the end of an evening. There's no desire to curl up against him and have him stay the night, to wake sleepy-eyed and warm next to him in the morning.

"Goodwife Manderson!" Jim Melville came up to her as they came off-stage after their final curtain, the applause of the audience still deafening. Alfred was here and there, praising and complimenting and exhorting people to please come to the next reading, they were doing a Shaw play next time, different costumes, different feel -

"Mr Melville."

"Now the play's over, you can take that dress home and burn it!" He smiled to cover his awkwardness.

"I might just do that, I've lived in it for so long now!"

"Here." He thrust a book at her. "This is for you. I have to say you were a fine goodwife, but you make a better ghost." And he was gone, out of the crowd of actors riding the adrenaline high of having done a fine performance. Someone popped a champagne cork, there was scattered applause. The sound of chairs and feet and voices reached them from beyond the curtain.

"Abby? I'll try and get you a bigger part next time." Alfred, close at her elbow, was looking at the book in her hand. "Walchurch ghosts. Where did that come from?"

"Jim Melville. He said I made a fine goodwife but a better ghost!"

"It seems you scared the superstitious old fool half to death twice, didn't you?"

"I did." Abby turned the pages slowly, accepted the glass of champagne, felt the bubbles hit her nose. I'll read it later.

Des was waiting for her outside the door, smiling, doffing a pretend hat.

"A true stage-door Johnny, that's me." He took her hand. "'Never thought I'd be waiting outside a theatre for someone! You were good, Abby."

"Thanks." She patted her bag. "Mr Melville, the

142

caretaker, gave me a book about Walchurch ghosts. He said I made a good ghost."

"You're getting quite a collection of Walchurch books." He grinned. "Come on, we're going for a meal to celebrate your success."

I hope that's all we're celebrating, thought Abby, with a touch of anxiety. I feel he's getting altogether too serious about me.

Over dinner, with the clink of silver on china, the murmur of voices, the rustle of linen - reminding Abby of her lunches with Kenneth Thompson and making her wonder why he hadn't called lately - Des asked:

"What are you doing about Christmas, Abby?"

"Christmas? That's two months away!"

"Only eight weeks, in fact. I wondered if you'd be going home at all."

"No. I left under a cloud. I shan't be going home."

"Not even for the festive season?"

She paused; knife and fork suspended above her plate, looking at the finely cooked food, wondering why she had a sudden craving for spit-roasted pig and boiled vegetables. Why the scent of mead and mulled wine should suddenly reach her. Why the dripping of greenery from stone walls should seem more desirable than paper decorations and tinsel.

"Not even for the festive season," she said, and went on eating.

"Would you ... spend Christmas with me?"

"Des." She rested her hands on the edge of the table, looked at him, saw the longing in his eyes and smiled. "Shall we decide nearer the time? Right now I've just been in a play, I've a ton of work at the office, I don't really know how I feel about Christmas or anything." And that's the truth, she thought, if you leave out Lord Josiah Danverson and his curled beard, his castle and his strength. Leave out the daydreams I keep having about him and the way I'm drawn to his tomb in the church. And I keep denying myself the sight of him, for it hurts to see him dead.

Hurts more than I thought it would. The memory brings a pang that is almost a physical pain.

"Okay. I'll ask you at the end of November."

"That will be better, I might have sorted myself out by then. You came as a surprise; I didn't intend to let anyone in my life!" She smiled to counter the statement, saw his answering grin, hoped she had possibly placated him for a while.

A couple at another table finished their meal, saw them, came over to talk. Friends from the party. Damn, thought Abby, smiling and joining in the conversation, if I'm not careful we'll be talked of as a couple and I don't want that.

What do you want?

I want to go back for Christmas.

The thought came with a jolt, made her almost spill her wine.

"Are you all right?" Concern lanced across the table. She nodded, said goodbye to the friends, turned back to Des.

"Fine, just a spasm. You know how it goes: too many tense muscles suddenly unlocking themselves."

"I know of a good way to unlock tense muscles." He grinned at her with a lascivious look. Abby grinned back. Tonight it would be fun to surrender to Des.

Partly, at least.

The flat felt warm. The heating had come on while they were out, giving a welcoming feel to the rooms for the first time in ages. Abby dropped her bag on the coffee table and turned to take Des in her arms.

"Now what was it you had in mind?" she whispered in his ear, feeling his tongue dart at her lips, his arms strong enough to lift her off the ground as he had done several times.

"I had this in mind." He touched his leather belt. Abby drew in a breath. Des had not tried that before; he had stuck to smaller things - her slipper, his hand, a plng-pong bat which had stung like crazy.

Fear shocked her to her hones. What if he isn't any good, what if the belt goes everywhere, what if - ?

There was only one way to find out. She kissed him again, took his hand and led him to the bedroom.

"Let me." He gestured at her clothes.

"Sure." She stood passive, raising and lowering arms, lifting and lowering her legs, letting him slowly disrobe her, lips and tongue everywhere, he found her nipples, her neck, her navel, her secret place, dry and cold right now. When he touched her shoulder she lay down and waited, scared, yet thrilled, clutching the coverlet with both hands.

"I've been practising," he told her, as if he had read her thoughts. She heard the whisper of leather leave material as it slid through the loops. A pause while he wrapped the buckle end around his hand. She felt a moment of pure apprehension before the belt landed with devastating force clear across both cheeks.

"Ouch!" she looked round, saw the devilish grin he wore, saw the belt fly through the air a second before it hit her again. Sight helped anticipation rush to meet the pain, causing an explosion of emotion. "You're hurting!" she gasped, struggling with herself to lie still, to take it. She knew she was getting wet immediately, felt the pain, longed for him to do it again.

"Of course." The belt landed again, nearer her thighs, she tossed her head in denial, cried out, but took it. The

145

leather landed again and then twice more.

"I think that'll do you," he murmured, pulling her toward him, examining the weals, running his hands over the hot flesh, letting his finger slide into her crack. She rolled on the bed, moaning.

"That'll do nicely," she tried to jest, longing to rub, wanting to keep the sting as long as she could, feeling the shock of the pain reach her toes and her innermost places. "You have been practising! Who with?"

"Not who - what." He rubbed gently, causing her to wince and then try to roll over. "Keep still, I want to look! I used a pillow and perfected my aim before attempting it on you. I didn't want the belt flying everywhere and nor would you!"

"Too right." She felt herself go even moister and then his fingers found her opening, found the sensitive pressure points, found her G spot.

The coupling was swift, almost savage in its intensity, Abby thrusting and writhing to gain every sensation she could, Des determined to pace her, to keep her going as long as he could. Abby wrapped her legs around his waist, urged him on with demanding thigh muscles, breathed in his musk and sweat, saw the tattoos close to her face and wondered fleetingly if she should question them, but let them blur as he moved against her, closing her eyes as they both exploded in simultaneous orgasms that left them shattered.

For a full ten minutes they lay still, exhausted, while Abby traced a finger down his back and he stayed with his eyes closed, his hands resting on her breast, occasionally tweaking a nipple.

"I'm beginning to get a feeling for what a dominant really goes through," he told her after a long silence in which their breathing was the only sound and movement to disturb the silent bedroom. "I'm now getting some pleasure out of actually beating you, my girl, so watch out!"

"Good," she breathed in his ear. "About time. You've had enough practice!"

"Talking of time, it's time I went home." He stirred, got up, and began to dress. Abby found some tissues and attempted to clean up some of the come, wondering why it was always such a messy afterglow. There has to be a way of having the glow without the mess!

She put on her robe, saw Des off and went to take a leisurely bath, letting the hot water soak away all her tensions. That had been good, but Des still had a long way to go. Still asking to do things, undress her, copping out at six. But then, he was a novice, she warned herself, still learning. He would appreciate her reaction tonight, it was the best love-making ever. With him.

Back in her bedroom, she slid under the duvet and picked up the ghost book, leafing through the pages almost idly, not really expecting to find anything, only wanting her thoughts side-tracked for a little while before finally giving way to sleep.

It seemed there were a lot of ghosts in Walchurch; the usual headless horseman passing the White Hart; an old lady who supposedly haunted the park and the lake, and was said to have drowned in the lake in 1811; a child said to have died while cleaning the chimney of Dane House. But these did not interest Abby. She turned the pages swiftly, looking for the lady in purple.

The King's Theatre cum-Community Centre has its own ghost, a lady from the time of Charles I.

On the site of the theatre was a castle belonging to Lord Danverson, a local dignitary and lord of the manor. The castle was destroyed by fire in 1750, but it did not stop the lady in purple from haunting the place. Various descriptions have been recorded. Overall it appears she has black hair caught up in a white cap and wears a flowing purple dress with a wide lace collar, very typical of the period. She is said to walk what were the walls of Danverson Castle, now incorporated into the theatre building. She walks as if trying to be silent, looking around her as she goes. She then climbs the stairs and disappears.

No one knows who the lady really is, or is supposed to be. One theory is that she was the wife of Lord Danverson and is perhaps searching for something.

Abby closed the book, marvelling at how a simple act like retrieving a dress from the past could create a legend.

She frowned, thinking over what she had just put into conscious thought,

To me, the travelling comes easy. I accept it as a fact of life. But if I were to tell anyone: Des, or friends at work, they'd think me insane. To travel back, to have sex with different men, to come back here again, would be a wonder to them. Now look, I've created a legend, a real ghost!

She got up, felt her bruises and smiled.

Good try, Des, good try, but you're nowhere near as good as your ancestor and never will be. He meant it, and he didn't stop at six, either. Nor would he!

I have to somehow wean you away from me, divert you to another path. You're not the man for me, much as I'd like to think you were.

You don't measure up to the men in the past.

I'd never hurt you, but ... You're no Lord Danverson and never will be ...

CHAPTER 28: THEN

The furniture glowed under the light of the afternoon sun, tassels, braids, covers, thick bulky furniture that looked as if it could only be moved by a strong man with strong arms.

The man stood by the window, gazing pensively out at the topiary and clipped yews. He wore a cut-away coat, waistcoat, stiff collar and cravat and had an expensive gold chain holding it all in place.

The room was heavy with the scent of pot pourri and the gathered blooms in the huge cut-glass vase on the polished table.

The man turned as Abigail approached. She almost caught her breath, for he was the identical twin of Alfred Fitzpaine.

"I didn't ring, did I?"

"No, Sir." She curtsied slightly, her heavy black dress scraping the floor, the white apron rustling stiff with starch.

"I don't remember seeing you here before. What's your name?"

"Brandon, Sir."

"Brandon, eh? From Walchurch?"

"Yes, Sir."

"New, are you?"

"Just arrived, Sir."

"So - what are you doing here?"

"To see if there was anything Sir needed."

"Nice of you. What have I done that you should be so attentive to my needs? Don't you have enough to do?"

"There's always enough to do here, Sir, but - "

"You came to see if there was something I needed. As it happens, there is." He slumped into a chair and waved a languid white hand at her. "A stiff drink, if you please, heavy on the whisky, light on the water."

"Sir." Abigail curtsied again and crossed swiftly to the large cabinet, finding the drinks easily - no doubt they had been moved to the front for easier access. Abigail thought Lord Fitzpaine? - had already consumed a few drinks this afternoon.

From outside came the sound of croquet mallets hitting the balls, cries of dismay or pleasure as a score was made or not made.

Will I score?

"Sir." She offered the whisky on a silver tray and stood back, waiting for approval or disapproval. He looked at her over the top of the glass, sipped the drink and nodded.

"It'll do." She turned to go but he called her back.

"Is Lady Fitzpaine eating with us?"

"I - I don't know for sure, Sir."

"Well, she wasn't that well at lunch, so perhaps it would be best if she ate in her room. In the meantime ..."

"Sir?"

"You seem vaguely familiar. You must have been here a while."

"No, Sir. Just arrived today."

"Strange. I could have sworn - "

"You might have seen me in Walchurch, Sir."

Come on, stop wasting time, thought Abigail desperately. Her thoughts must have reached him for he drained the glass in one swallow and put it down.

"Come."

"Where to, Sir?"

"Wherever I say."

She followed him through the ornate hallway, hung with rich curtains and brooding portraits. A profusion of dead animals poked their heads through the walls, mute displays of prowess with guns.

The stairs were smooth, polished dark with age and use, banister carved in flowing scrolls. They passed a maid who stood back, eyes downcast, who greeted them with a small curtsey and a muttered 'Lord Albert' as they went by. "Staff these days at least know how to keep their place," commented Lord Albert, throwing the words over his shoulder casually. Abigail smothered a smile.

Albert. Alfred. Close enough. What if I were to tell him his descendant is a pompous accountant who becomes a human being only when he gets into a theatre and has a bunch of contrary and often turbulent amateur actors to direct?

"If you're really not busy I have something I'd like to do this afternoon."

The door of a bedroom was thrown open. Inside lay the opulence of gilt and brocade, rich carpeting, tasselled beaded hangings, silk bedcover, mirrors everywhere. 'Her' mirror was over the hearth. Abigail moved carefully around it, not wanting to be thrown back to the future, not yet.

"I'm taking it for granted you know why we're here," he said, stripping clothes off so fast it was a wonder they didn't tear. Good tailoring, thought Abigail, as she unbuttoned her dress.

"Of course, Sir."

"And you don't mind?"

"Why else am I here?" she murmured, stepping out of the dress and leaving it in a crumpled black heap, a shadow by the side of the bed.

He walked over to her, gripped both her arms, slid them around his neck, lifted her, pushed her back against a wall for support and fumbled with his cock, sliding it, ramming it into her dry, unready body. Abigail automatically locked her legs around his waist, held on

151

while he pumped away at her, worrying about this one. No foreplay, no anticipation, not even so much as a kiss!

It was all too fast. Within seconds of entering her, he came, lifting her up and letting her almost fall to the ground. She stood still, saying nothing, not daring to move, not daring to think that was all she had come back for; that few seconds of feeling.

Then he looked down at her and sneered.

"Not a movement, not a flicker from you." She watched him closely, detecting a familiar lustful look "Right, what do I need to do to make you react to me? Hmm?" He walked around her, poking her breast, her cheeks, her arms. "Insolence! Not a movement, not a reaction to me! I know, I have just the thing for you."

"But, Sir - " Abigail cut off the word when she saw his grim look. Obviously he had expected more, but hadn't given her the chance to do it.

He crossed the room, pale buttocks jiggling in the late afternoon sun, his cock growing hard again as he rummaged in a drawer. Abigail watched with growing apprehensions as he exclaimed "Ah-ha!" and turned, holding a small plaited dress whip in his hand. "For those who dare to come brazen into a man's bedroom, even by invitation! A severe beating, don't you think?"

Abigail was speechless. She hadn't experienced a whip before - she had no idea whether she could stand it.

"Lie down." She still hesitated, watching as he produced cords from another drawer. "I won't ask you to be still, I'll make sure you lie still. Now, lie down!"

She lay on the silk coverlet, feeling the chill silk against her skin, the roughness and tightness of the cord as he bound her wrists and ankles to the bedhead and the legs. He muttered as he worked, mouthing curses about insolent sluts who come to work for the upper classes and expected to be treated like equals, those who didn't appreciate a good man when they had one, whether he be employer or not.

Abigail kept very quiet, felt her usual apprehension and anticipation creeping over her, knowing she would regret this particular trip, but at the same time sexily aware how much she anticipated it, even as she feared a new, brainstorming, experience.

A long moment of silence, of stillness, of waiting ...

"Right, young woman." And the whip came down, across her back, half across her cheeks, bringing a shriek of pain such as she had never experienced before. She screamed out loud.

"Silence!" he shouted at her, whipping her again and again, but Abigail couldn't be silent, it hurt far too much. She fought the bonds, shouted and screamed as the whip descended time and again, cutting her back, her thighs, her bottom.

"I said silence!" he shouted, pushing her head down into the covers. Abigail bit the silk, let tears flow and sobbed as silently as she could while be vented his apparent anger on her, whip slashing down anywhere, with no sense, no timing, no rhythm.

Finally it appeared to be over. The bonds were taken off and she was allowed to roll over, to cry properly.

Abigail lay very still, smarting everywhere, crying, tears coursing down her neck onto the silk, staining it a dark colour.

Lord Albert Fitzpaine stood staring at her, his cock harder than ever, at least half as thick again as it had been first time around.

Abigail held out her arms, feeling nothing but pain everywhere, not an apparent trace of eroticism left. But still she needed him, needed that cock, that release. He fell onto the bed, climbed over to her, parted her legs with rough hands, gaped at the naked mound, and sighed as she reached for him. This time he did stop to kiss her, whisky breath and white teeth, tongue with a taste of spirit and a spirit which sent him thrusting deep into her waiting body.

"Damn me if you didn't enjoy it!" he whispered, muffled, his lips pressed against her thick black curls.

Then they thrust and rolled against one another, Abigail raising her hips clear off the bed, giving herself over to the release, the pain dying back, the sheer afterglow taking every part of her. She caught at his body with her nails, bit his neck and shoulder, cried out in passion.

The silk let them slide. They moved up the bed against the headboard. Abigail found herself again impaled on his cock, legs around his waist, being lifted clear off the bed, his face in her breasts, loving every moment of it, flowing to let him push against her.

When it was over, an eternity later, he lay on one side, propped up on an elbow, looking at her with a puzzled frown. "You enjoyed it," he said again.

"Not the whipping, Sir, no. But the afterwards, well, that was - "

"I know. I need to hurt someone to get like it and the damn women around here won't let me, bunch of milksops! But you - "

This was not the time or the place to discuss it.

"I'll need to get back to my duties, Sir."

"Of course. Cook will be wondering where you've gone, not to mention Mrs Mathers."

"If you don't mind, Sir, I'll just get dressed - "

She struggled into the underclothes and the long black dress as he lay still and watched her, afternoon sun lighting up his white body, his long muscled legs, his magnificent manhood. For a fleeting moment she

154

wondered if the current Alfred Fitzpaine was that well hung and how she could find out.

Then she picked up her apron and cap and walked over to the mirror.

CHAPTER 29: NOW

The school-days one was fun, in a strange sort of way. By 'one' I mean one of my travels, of course. I'd read so much in the magazines about the school scenes, the cane, gym-slips, the headmaster, the school desk, I had to do something, I had to try it! Couldn't call myself an s/m person without trying the basic scene.

Did I like it?

No.

The school outfit felt wrong, out of place on an adult, I didn't like the bossing about in the school, didn't like being told what to do any more. Too independent, too proud. (What would Lord Danverson say about that?)

I didn't mind the caning, although it was a good deal harder than anything I'd had before, but then, I say that about a lot of things.

Anyway, I borrowed a school outfit from the theatre, looked in my mirror, went back to the school I attended. I never remembered it being so... lonely. The long empty corridors, the awful school smell, toilets, chalk, bodies. Mr Lloyd was as awful as I remembered, the instant way he assumed I was being sent for punishment, his complete taking over.

I waited outside a class, feeling stupid and helpless, wondering why I just didn't walk off, but there was always the problem of the mirror, finding the damn mirror. It wasn't in the school, I could sense that. So I had no choice but to stay, to take whatever was coming and then come back.

He'd had time to think about me, and took me to his home, the better to avoid detection. I had a sneaking suspicion which proved to be true. He used contact magazines and advertised his services, and - heaven help me - people came for his cane.

I slipped up, though, thinking I'd get the traditional six of the best. I got 12. And boy, did they hurt! He made every one tell, every one a distinct line of pure pain that cut like nothing else. I knew I'd had them.

I wish there'd been a way to see his face when I never came back down the stairs! There he was with car outside, goodness-knows-what hiding in his trousers and me disappeared off the face of the earth!

Abby suddenly became impatient with her commentary, covered her typewriter, shrugged into a coat and set off for the church.

Something was calling her; something that could not be ignored.

Chapter 30: Now

The church door creaked, protesting at being asked to open, swung back on the huge iron hinges and allowed Abby to enter. A cold north light filtered through the windows, grey, depressing.

The altar was draped in purple, flowers had disappeared from the ornate pedestal stands. Everything had an air of waiting or mourning or something. Abby flicked through the pages of the parish magazine idly, catching sight of the list of Advent services.

Advent. Waiting. Of course - no flowers, deep purple, the white would replace it for Christmas when the whole church would be a blaze of light, flowers, joyful anticipation of the birth of Christ.

Advent.

Waiting.

That's what I'm doing.

But not any more.

Ahead of her, the Danverson Chapel. No covers any more, no bricks, no tarpaulin. Walls had been repainted, water stains vanished, everything looked new and clean and fresh.

She approached slowly, almost as if it were Josiah Danverson himself lying so still, awaiting burial. Where is he buried? she asked herself. Where is the actual skeleton, where is-?

Beneath the tomb, of course. Deep beneath the tomb, safe, where no one can reach him.

She searched for and found the light switch, the figures springing to life in the cold gold light.

Gentle fingers traced the outline of Lord Danverson's face, felt the curl of the beard, touched his strong hands, lingered the length of his body, smart in doublet and hose.

My man. My chosen man. Better than all the rest, better than anyone I've met, here or in the past. Now I can - for the first time - look at your wife.

The chairs had gone from the back of the monument. There was nothing between the table tomb and the wall, which held a glass case protecting brass effigies of other Danversons, more notable figures. Abby couldn't at that moment think who they were, her whole attention was being drawn to the figure alongside Josiah Danverson.

It was her.

The oval face, the cluster of curls, although ivory cream now, could just as easily be black, her rose-bud mouth, her long fingers clasped lightly on her breast in the classic pose of the sleeping dead.

With legs that threatened to betray her, that wanted to buckle somewhere around the knees, she moved closer; looked down at her sleeping self, touched the chill stone, traced the folds of her robe, the gold pendant at the waist, the thick choker round her neck.

Me.

That's me.

Then her knees did give way as a coldness swept over her, drowning all emotions, blinding her eyes with unshed tears. She slumped to the floor alongside the tomb, where the inscription stared at her, defying her to ignore the message.

ABIGAIL GUINEVERE DANVERSON
Beloved wife of Josiah Thomas Danverson
Lord of the Manor
Died 20th May 1673
Mourned by her children and all who knew her
For Love and for Glory

Abby sat on the cold tiles, shivering with more than

cold. There was her name, her date of death, just three days after her husband. Fever? Broken heart? Why didn't she survive him?

It is me.

The thought would not go away.

Coincidence.

No way.

Abigail Guinevere Danverson, lying there alongside Josiah Thomas Danverson, the man who occupied almost all her waking thoughts and most of her dreams.

The man she now knew and recognised that she loved beyond all reason and sense, beyond herself and her life.

Did the mirror only operate for me? Was I the only one who could go back in time through its silver face? Others said it didn't reflect what they wanted but it didn't transfer them as it did me.

Because I was being prepared for this moment.

Because if I don't go back, the circle will be broken and goodness knows what would happen to the pattern of life! I'm in a time loop.

I have been guided here through the mirror. I have learned to appreciate the pleasure-pain syndrome so that Josiah can beat me and I will love it and please him.

I have been led towards feeling right in the dress of the period, towards knowing the outline of the castle which will be my home. I have been guided towards this moment, this revelation.

"Are you all right, my dear?" The vicar's kindly face peered over the figures, concerned, worried. "I saw someone come in. I couldn't see you at first, then I realised the Danverson Chapel light was on."

"Yes." She struggled to stand up, held on to her own effigy's feet. "I was reading the inscription down here. It was the only way to see it."

She came around the tomb, looked back just once with longing at her own face and his, and then looked defiantly towards the purple-clad altar.

"An odd inscription, I think." He clasped his hands, rubbed them together, the chill of the ancient stones reaching out to encompass them both. "A reversal of the Danverson motto."

"You know we did a play at the King's Theatre recently, called For Glory And For Love?" He nodded and she went on: "while we were doing it - I was in it, by the way, playing a small part - I wondered if the motto could be reversed, to be "For Love and for Glory", because being a woman I would put the love first. And then I found it here."

"Must have been an odd feeling for you."

"It was." More than you'll ever know.

He looked towards the figure, then back at her.

"And Lady Danverson looks -"

"Just like me. I know, I just saw that. Gave me a shock."

"What a coincidence!"

"Not helped by the fact that my name is the same as hers, too. I'm Abigail." She left off the Guinevere, that would be too much to take. She decided to change the subject. "The church looks very empty right now."

"I always think Advent is such an exciting time; the preparation, the waiting." He moved away from the Danverson Chapel. "Then we have the joy of Christmas. I think Lady Danverson must have felt that too. Here." He switched on another light, and charity boards flared into view. "Lady Danverson endowed £5 a year to be given to the church for decoration at Christmas and £20 for the poor of the parish to be clothed and fed in the cold weather. She must have been a very kind-hearted lady. Twenty pounds was a terrific amount of money then."

I have so much to remember, she told herself. So much to take back with me. Was that me donating that money? I have to find out.

"I'll leave you to read the board. It goes on a bit. There are a lot of other benefactors mentioned here. Later Lord Danverson endowed money. It all sort of disappeared over the years, unfortunately, but still, it was a good thought and must have helped a lot of people at the time. Will you be coming to Christmas services?"

"I don't know if I'll be here," she said in all honesty. "If am, I will."

"Good, good. I must go, lots to do, you know, pastoral visits at this time of year ..."

"Thank you."

Abby turned back to the boards, read the ancient wording in its fine script which was also familiar to her. The Danversons had donated money through the years, her descendants had done well by the parish.

But only if I go back and start it all off, or none of this exists.

She was alone in the church with her thoughts and decisions. No one to see her. She went back to the tomb and touched Lord Danverson's hand.

"Hold on, I'm coming." To her own image she whispered: "I won't let you down, I'm coming."

With a determined set to her chin, Abby left the church, letting the door swing shut behind her, shutting out the cold but not the memories of seeing her face carved in stone, seeing her motto and her name carved in flowing script on base of the tomb. Must have been a broken heart, she decided. If I love him as much as I think I'm going to, then I would surely die without him.

Well, get going, girl, there's one hell of a lot to do. Job to quit, flat to tidy and pack away, notice to give, people to notify. Why should I? Why don't I just go?

Pack the belongings, label them for parents. They'll never understand. If I was to go and say goodbye they'd never understand. They'd turn their cold faces to me, cold as the stone I just left.

What do I do about Des?

I'll work on that.

She hurried down the flagstoned path, determined to get going on the thousand-and-one things to do before she looked in the mirror for the very last time.

"Abby, there's something I want to say, to ask." Des shifted uncomfortably on her settee, pushed a cushion behind leaned forward and began to fiddle with the magazines on coffee table.

"Go on." She sipped coffee, looked at him over the rim the mug, wondering what was coming next. Somehow she had to distance herself from Des, and hoped this was the opportunity.

"I've ... been offered a chance to go to Canada with the firm."

"Congratulations! I'm sure you'll love it."

"I was afraid you'd say that. You'd not think of coming with me, then."

"No." She said it very gently, hoping he wouldn't mind much. "I don't think I'd like to leave England right now." Isn't that the truth?"

"I thought you'd say that. I accepted the job, knowing I'd probably go alone." He looked sad yet at ease with himself. "Well, I had a feeling it was all one-sided here, anyway."

"It was, Des, I'm truly sorry. I like you an awful lot but-"

"Not love. Well, there it is. I might find myself some little Canadian girl!"

"I hope you do."

"No point in asking if I might write, is there?"

"Listen." She put down her coffee, leaned forward and took his hand. "You've been great, a wonderful lover. I've enjoyed being with you, in and out of bed! It was fun going to classes with you, having dinner and everything, but don't hang on to me, Des. If you write, you'll be hanging on to see if I change my mind, and that won't do. Let go, start a new life out there, see what happens, who comes along. Someone out there will love you more than I can."

"You're right, of course you are. Well, thanks, Abby; it's been good. I think I'll go now, if that's all right?"

"Sure. Anything you want. Do take care. I'll never forget you."

"Good. That's something to hold on to." He kissed her lightly and then gathered her in his arms, kissing her long and hard. "God, I wish you were coming!"

Gently she disengaged herself. "I can't, Des, truly I can't. It wouldn't work. And it would be far worse to have a relationship break up in another country. For both of us! But I'm really flattered you asked me."

"All right. Well, take care, Abby, whatever you do."

The door closed behind him.

Abby walked around the room, straightening cushions, putting her magazines in the rack, sipping cold coffee, feeling very sad. It was a shame; it might have worked, in another time and in another place, if only she hadn't been so sure her destiny lay somewhere else, with another man.

This clinched her decision, one she had been approaching for some time, one that had been inexorably drawing her towards it.

"One last adventure," she told herself, half-turning toward her mirror. "Just one. And then I promise I'm going back forever. I want to hear minstrels playing, I want to see the castle, I want to be with the dogs, especially that lovely bitch ..."

She went to her wardrobe where she had hidden a dress to take her back, changed nylon and lace for undies, pulled the dress on and then spent fifteen minutes with heating tongs curling her hair into tight, tight curls. When she was ready she went towards the mirror.

"If nothing else, it'll help me forget Des' sad face!" And she glanced in the glass.

Chapter 32: Then

Dane House stood dreaming under an October sky, a blue so cold it almost hurt, the sun sparkling from gable windows, the slightest of breezes disturbing the dead leaves on the beeches as they shivered with the first hint of winter.

Abigail stood on the gravelled path, her heavy wedge heels and platform soles sinking into the shifting pebbles. Prim and proper, her dress was a round-necked decorous knee-length floral print, her hair twisted into curls, tight curls, as if permed. Very forties, she told herself; I hope that's where I am. One last adventure. One last Happening. I hope it's a really, really good one.

After this it's -

"Have you come for the game?" A male voice. She spun round, almost overbalancing on the shifting gravel.

"Yes," she told the smiling Brylcreemed young man. His dark hair was cut close to his head, he wore a short-sleeved shirt, baggy shorts, and plimsolls. He was tanned, athletic and good-looking. Instantly fanciable. She moved a step towards him, feeling the treacherous gravel give way. "I am at the right place, aren't I?"

"Dane House, that's right. What's your name?"

"Abigail."

"I'm Ralph." He took her arm, escorted her onto the grass, where it was easier to walk. "I hope you brought some clothes?"

"Well, no, because no one told me what to expect!"

He grinned, sudden gleam of pure white well-maintained expensive teeth. Rare in this time.

"Janet will have something you can change into, I'm sure. After all, you won't need much, will you? Come on."

Abigail followed as he set off at a fast pace, crossing

lawns and huge sweep of gravel before the large porch, elegant columns and elaborate facade. The door stood open, allowing the cool October air into the hall. Abigail caught the swift scent of money and then they were inside, surrounded by panelling that reminded her of Sir Anthony's London Club, then up the stairs, passing huge windows which ended in cushioned window seats. She looked out across vast areas of green fringed with trees, caught exciting glimpses of a pool, perhaps a lake, dark blue and glittery cold.

"Janet!" Ralph banged on the door with a fist, smiling at Abigail as he did so. "Someone's here for the game, needs some suitable clothes!"

"I'll be right there!"

Ralph stood aside. "I'll see you later then, all right?"

"Sure." Abigail trembled from head to foot, wondering what she had let herself in for. It could be good, it could be bad. Either way it promised to be an experience. What sort of game could it possibly be?

Janet was a short tubby girl with bright blue eyes, a doll-like face and an engaging laugh. She was wearing tennis shorts, baggy enough to almost hide her thick thighs, and a floppy shirt, not baggy enough to hide full pendulous breasts. Abigail could almost feel the sensuality radiating from her. She smiled while looking puzzled.

"I don't know you, do I?"

"No." Abigail fought for a name, and found one. "Anne said if I came along I could be a part of the game, but she didn't tell me any more."

"Anne? Oh you mean Anne St John?"

Abigail nodded. She didn't, but that didn't matter. Janet's face cleared. "Oh yes, I remember telling her about it at darling D'Arcy's engagement party." Janet rolled her eyes in her head and fluttered her hands. "Such a gorgeous man out of circulation! What are we going to do? Come in, come in."

Abigail entered the frilled, lacy room, and was overwhelmed by perfume and sheer girliness. A huge canopied bed occupied most of the space, hung with delicate lace, trimmed with pink bows. Clothes were draped here and there over a printed screen, on the back of a spindly-legged chair, on the floor. The whole room shouted 'female' and was too cutesy cute for her liking. Janet walked around the obstacles, talking about the fine day they had for the game, who was coming ... Abigail caught some names but they passed on by. She hoped they would come back when she met the people who wore the names. Janet was flaunting her bust as if she were a figurehead for a large ocean-going wooden ship. It made her feel inadequate. Her breasts were small compared to this Amazon.

"Now, do you know what we have to do?"

"No, not really. Anne wasn't very specific."

"Well, she wouldn't be." Janet sank down on a cushioned window seat, pushed the floral drapes aside and looked out across the fields. "Well, we're hounds, us girls. There's going to be six of us altogether. We get a head start on the guys, and what guys!" Again the eye-rolling and hand fluttering. Abigail presumed from that the men would be hunky and good-looking: at least she hoped they would be. "We have all the grounds to roam in, and you know how big they are! So we can go where we like, run where we like, but if we're caught, we have to pay a forfeit. Then we're free again." Smiling, deeply sexual, very telling. "I think they've devised some wonderful forfeits for us girls. I'm glad you could make it, what's your name?' She got up again, burrowing around in her wardrobe.

"Abigail. "

"Right - Abigail. Here's some plimsolls, I think they'll fit you. And a top and some shorts. That's all you'll need. Then we gather in the porch ready for the off!"

"Sounds great!" Said with all the enthusiasm Janet had shown, almost gushing. Not Abigail's style at all but it seemed appropriate.

"John's arranged for some Yanks to come along too!" Janet looked in her full-length mirror. "God, what I'd give to get off with a Yank, get him to take me back to the States out of this drab dull land!"

"It'll be all right when the rationing's over."

"Sure it will, but how long do we have to wait? I'd kill for some new nylons. A cat laddered my last pair, and the coupons don't go anywhere, do they?"

"Well, no." Abigail sat on the end of the bed, putting on the plimsolls, reluctant to change her dress in front of Janet and wondering why. In the end she decided she was being stupid, but still blushed as she pulled the dress over her head, glad she had thought to change her underclothes for the cotton items instead of the lace-and-nylon ones she had worn that morning.

After all her fears, Janet never even looked at her.

Dressed in the shorts and top, Abigail felt at least up to running. The dress had been somewhat hindering, even to walk in, she had to concede that.

Even if it did give her a problem, she had to come back to change out of the shorts and plimsolls and get her dress and shoes back. And she had to find the mirror which wasn't here, not in Janet's elaborately feminine room.

"Here they are!" Janet leapt up, grabbed Abigail's hand and began to tow her towards the door. Abigail had time to see a jeep swing into the space in front of the house, saw some young men with huge smiles pile out and then they were running along the corridor, down the carpeted stairs and into the hall.

"Hi, gang!" The men clustered on the porch, shouting jokes at one another in English and strong American accents, slapping backs and shoulders, smiling at Janet and the stranger with her. Abigail began to blush, wondering why she should do that every time someone looked at her.

"Hey, a newcomer! Who brought you along?" They pushed closer, admired her hair, one of them letting a curl slide round his finger, another running a thumb down her face.

"Anne St John sent her along." Janet hung on the arm of a dark-haired man who looked down at her with smiling eyes.

"Good, we needed a new face."

"Where's everyone else?" Even as the blond man spoke, another car drew up behind the jeep and four girls got out. Abigail watched them come towards her, elegant in smart suits, tight dresses, hats and heeled shoes. She felt a bit out of place, but then realised they, too, would have to change into the same outfit. Fair's fair. Those of us playing a game of hunt, all have to have the same clothes on.

"Hello there!"

Janet took Abigail's arm.

"This is Joy, here's Maria, the blonde there is Marilyn and that's Patsy." Abigail nodded to them all. "This is Abigail. She was sent along by Anne St John, who obviously isn't coming."

"No, she can't make it - indisposed, and we know what that means, don't we? But she didn't say she would send anyone else." Marilyn shrugged. "Not that it matters, we need six for the game, don't we, guys?"

"Sure do." Ralph took over the introductions. "John, Martin, our two American cousins, Barry and Gareth

170

and over there, Damien, who thinks he's too good for us, doesn't he?"

A dark-haired man sat gloomily on a stone bench by a fountain throwing water out of a dolphin's mouth. He had his back half-turned to them.

Gareth moved closer to Abigail, his dark-hued skin tanned as if he had been in the sun for too long, gleaming white teeth and very pink gums. Very well fed and cared for, thought Abigail, despite the shortages; but then the Americans didn't seem to go short.

"Damien's all right," he said in a heavy accent she couldn't quite place, but thought might be Southern. "He just needs his own company now and then. But he likes the game, doesn't he, Jan?"

"That he does." She turned back to Abigail. "You got the rules all right? The guys set the forfeits. Could be - well, be prepared for anything from being dunked in the pond, to-"

"To being fucked." Ralph took her arm. "I'm sorry to be crude but we need to know you're game before we start, don't we guys? We don't need anyone shouting rape afterwards."

The other women stood staring, curious, waiting for a response. Abigail felt out of place, the complete stranger, at that moment. The breeze touched her with ice-cold fingers. Apprehension? Sexual excitement? Fear of the unknown? All that, and more.

"I'm game."

Everyone smiled.

"Good for you." That was Joy, with a genuinely friendly grin to go with it. They went past Janet into the house, obviously to change. Abigail watched them go, envying their money and their self-assurance.

"Go talk to Damien, he hasn't met you yet." Gareth pushed her gently and she set off across the gravel feeling very conspicuous. They no doubt wanted to talk about her while she was safely out of earshot.

Damien appeared half-asleep, resting against the back of stone bench, his eyes heavy-lidded and sultry, his mouth pressed in a hard, almost cruel line.

"Damien? I'm Abigail, they said to come and meet you."

"Hello there. I don't think you've been here before; I would have remembered you." He sat up, extended a hand, drew her dawn on the coolness beside him. "You know what we do?"

"Of course. Janet spelt it out and what she didn't make clear, Ralph did."

"He would. Well- " He let his finger run down her arm, making the hair stand up, 'you're a fine-looking girl. I'll enjoy finding you." The hand clasped her wrist tightly, making the skin go white. She clenched her teeth against the sudden pain, not letting him see he was hurting her. This man would give the other thing she had come for. On the other hand, as this was to be her last adventure, wouldn't a simple fucking do?

No.

"Okay everyone!" Ralph was calling, obviously in charge of the proceedings for the day at least. Damien got up, held out his hand to Abigail and led her back to the group.

Now the women were all wearing the same thing, shorts, tops and running shoes. Ralph held up a watch, glanced at it, looked around and grinned.

"Fifteen minutes, that's all you've got, now go!"

They scattered in all directions, Abigail making for the side of the house, panicking, wondering if there were out-buildings she could use for a hiding place until she got the lie of the land. If the others had played this game before, they knew where they were going. She didn't.

A stable, smelling of fresh horse and old straw. Abigail slipped round a half door, crouched down so no one could see her head above the top of it, burrowed among the straw bales, and sat down to rest and think.

Six men.

Six different forfeits, or did they all want the same thing? She could hear voices, screams that sounded more like pleasure than terror, shouts of laughter and a few calling out names just to see what would happen. She heard hers among them but didn't move.

Anticipation surged through her, strong enough to make her worry about dampening the shorts. The mirror had heard her request for a good one this time, a real adventure, if ever there was one! Six men, six chances of getting what she wanted - and more - before ...

A face appeared at the door, shadowy, indistinct. A body slipped into the stable.

"Abigail? I'm sure I saw you come in here." Damien, looking for her. Damien with the cruel mouth. She stayed very still. Suddenly he pounced on her hiding place, caught her wrist and dragged her free.

"I knew I'd find you here, it's the first place all newcomers go for." He pulled her to him, kissed her cruelly hard. She felt her lips plastered back against her teeth, felt his probing tongue, felt herself responding, her arms sliding around her neck, her body grinding against his.

"Your forfeit is a roll in the hay with me," he told her, pushing her down on the straw bales.

"My pleasure is to roll in the hay with you," she told him, pulling at his shoulders, drawing him down on top of her.

And it was. Already she was moist, ready for anything. He pulled at her shorts and cotton panties, threw them to one side, allowed his fingers to find her clit, pressed hard and sent her writhing in ecstasy almost immediately. With her top out of the way, he found a breast with his free hand, rubbing a nipple which came erect. Abigail found his buttons, pushed his shorts out of the way and allowed her fingers to run the length and width of his cock, longing for it, wondering if she should go for it immediately.

There was no decision to be made. He was on top of her, pressing her down onto the sharp needles of straw, kicking his shorts out of the way and plunging deep into her. "You're one of the most willing we've had for ages," he muttered into her hair, kissing her neck, thrusting deep into her with every word. "Sometimes they play coy, but not you!"

Abigail said nothing, just pulled his body, grabbed his buttocks in both hands, feeling the muscles, feeling the firmness, pulling him harder and harder into her.

He rocked backwards and forwards, kissed her neck, her eyes, her shoulders, bit at the soft skin of her breasts, soared with her on the heights of passion, her legs locked irrevocably around his slim muscular body. The explosion came instantly, and perfectly together.

A moment, thought Abigail, a moment to relish the feeling. But there were no moments. Damien looked down at her, rolled off, pushed her clothes over her naked body.

"No time to rest, you have to keep going, someone else might want you! And if they feel about you as I do, they will!"

"You were good." She spoke while struggling into the panties and shorts again, pulling her top down, pushing at her curls.

"Go!" he pushed her towards the door. "And if I find you again, there'll be a different forfeit, believe me!"

With a shiver of apprehension and excitement, Abigail

crept out of the door. She could hear and see no one, so she took a chance, rushing across the beautifully kept lawns towards the trees and summer-house she could see. Her legs felt weak. She wanted to lie down somewhere for half an hour, but somehow she kept going, breath pumping, arms swinging, getting a surge of emotion, of pleasure, from the mere act of jogging.

A mistake. The summer-house was a mistake. If she'd had time to think, she would have realised it was an obvious place for the hounds to go.

"I should have thought," she told herself, dismayed, as Ralph appeared from the back of the building, smiling broadly. "I did want time to unwind a little!" But the power of the game, the hunt, was with her now and she didn't mind that much, not really; this was pleasure, this was pure emotion, this hunting and being hunted, being found, being set free to run again.

Whoever devised such a wonderful game knew what they doing, understood the psychology of s/m, even if it was never expressed in words.

"Caught you!"

"You have," she agreed, standing obediently and waiting him to decide what her forfeit was.

A shriek split the air from another part of the grounds, laughter and the sound of revelling.

"Sounds like someone else has been caught, too." Ralph smiled, looking her up and down. "Now, I wonder what might be appropriate for someone like you?"

"What does that mean?" She raised her eyes carefully to his face, saw the considering look, wondered if he had seen her for what she was, a submissive.

Wondered if these well-bred and monied people would know of the longings she had.

Why not? They're human under the money, she thought.

"I think a good spanking ought to sort you out," he said, drawing her into the summer-house.

It held the scents of summer, the perfume of flowers, growing things, of warm evenings and cool nights, of sun-splashed dawns.

It also held a convenient bench, set at just the right height.

Abigail stood, breathing in the apprehension that surged through her, watching Ralph look her up and down. She turned at his command, let him trail his hands over hips, obeyed his next command to go over his knees. He had hard legs; they bored into her body. The floor was hard and she didn't want to tumble onto it, so she lay there, helpless and sexy, awaiting his next move.

"And I'll use one of these." He stripped a plimsoll from her foot and held it firmly by the heel. Abigail strained back to see what he was doing, saw a smile that meant only one thing - he was a man who enjoyed it.

Then the plimsoll was being brought down with strength onto her upturned bottom, covered only by cotton knickers and the thin shorts Janet had provided.

"Oh dear, they're leaving a mark. I'll have to get rid of that." And he did it even harder.

He was quick, a veritable rain of smacks which stung almost unbearably, the plimsoll's rubber sole rebounding from her tight skin and clothes. He was so thorough hardly an area was left untouched. Abigail writhed and struggled despite her best intentions, feeling Damien's juices ooze into her panties, feeling her own juices flowing despite her feeling distinctly uncomfortable. The plimsoll was leaving an indelible impression on her cheeks. The more she struggled the more Ralph held her firmly, one arm around her waist, the other doing its best to ensure she was properly spanked.

Finally, he helped her up, red-faced and puffing from the length of time she had been flattened over two very strong muscled thighs and knees. She stood, rubbing at her hot cheeks, wondering if he wanted anything else of her for the forfeit, hoping he did, yet wanting time to absorb the feelings.

"You'll do," he told her, looking her up and down again. "Now, go!"

It was hard to run, to dodge and disappear round trees when your bottom aches and burns from the results of an expert spanking. Abigail looked back towards the house, bathed in late afternoon sunshine and ran straight into Gareth, standing waiting in a copse of trees.

"Ah, the lovely English rose, with her dark hair and fair skin!" He drawled his words, making them sound almost exotic. "I'm pleased you ran into me." He encircled her waist with a strong arm, drew her down onto the thick covering of leaves and bracken. Abigail registered the softness of mosses, the delicate scent of musty decay and animal life, before her mouth and her senses were full of this strong American cousin. His kisses were fiery, his tongue sharp and inviting, his hands quick and supple, finding all her erogenous zones without any hesitation. Her shorts were again removed, he cupped her cheeks and felt their heat.

"You ran into our friend Ralph." He ran his hands over the redness, making her wince. "There's more to come, if you're the last one to be found!"

"I don't - " He kissed her, silencing her words.

"You'll find out. Now, roll over!"

"Whatever and wherever." Abigail rolled over, raised herself up on her knees, rested her head on her arms and let him look at her, tried again to ask what he meant about the end of the game.

"I don't... " but he was entering her, feeling her body

expand to accommodate his thick cock, feeling his fingers seek and then find her dripping clit, the two sensations together creating waves of feeling that were hard to contain. Pressure on nerves already sensitive and almost raw, excitement flooded her, she panted hard pushed her sore bottom back against him, felt the warmth of the spanking still there, felt it all build, came once, twice and then a third time before he exploded into her.

She slumped face down as he withdrew. That in itself was a thrill, twigs and leaves pressing into her bust, her navel, her stomach. Gareth smoothed her curls, ran a hand down her back, caressed the still-red cheeks.

"Wow, couldn't I do with a babe like you in my home!" he was obviously admiring. Abigail smothered a smile in her curls, playing with a frond of bracken, letting the exquisite after-orgasm feeling swamp her.

"Stay put until the bell goes." He slapped her hard, got up, adjusted his shorts and strode away, strong and tall in the late afternoon sun. The gentle lethargy changed to sleep. Abigail dozed, the only sound the call of birds and the occasional whisper of leaves from the trees above and around her.

A bell tolled, sending its mournful sound across the lawns and fields, across the lake and into the trees, where birds took flight at the disturbance, shrieking their annoyance into the cooling night air.

Abigail woke with a start, wondering where she was and how much time had gone by.

"Stay put until the bell goes." Gareth's parting words. She got up slowly, stretched aching muscles, dusted debris from her clothes and began to walk out of the copse, half-dazed, remembering she was at Dane House, wondering if the game was over and what Gareth had meant by the last person to be found.

Damien appeared from out of the shadows, startling

her. He grabbed her wrists and bound them behind her back with cord, pulling it tight, tying what felt like elaborate knots.

"I said I'd have a different forfeit if I caught you again." He drew her close to him. "You're a strange person, Abigail. I somehow feel you are not quite here, that any moment now you will disappear into thin air! Now, why should I feel like that?"

"I have no idea." She pulled at her bonds. "Tied, I can't go anywhere!"

"I know. That's why I tied you."

"I've enjoyed the game, Damien, a lot." The evening was cool now, purpling sky, birds circling wearily over Dane House which was now a large block of shadow pierced with spots of gold, rather like a memory.

"It isn't over yet. The bell just told everyone that the game is officially ended, except for the last rites."

"I rather guessed that, from something Gareth said."

"There is always a finale and you've become the candidate for today."

"A finale? What sort of finale?"

"Do you want it spelt out in advance, or should I let you find out? Well, no, I'll tell you." They stood in the rapidly darkening evening, gnats and midges dancing around them, the sky turning a darker purple-black under clouds that began to bank up on the horizon. Abigail felt cold and didn't think it was entirely due to the evening closing in.

"The last one to be found is the one we have for the finale. And you were the last one to walk back on to the lawn."

"Because Gareth said stay put till the bell rings."

Damien laughed. "Of course, he tricked you into being the last one! Now, you know that large elm standing on the edge of the lawn there?'

She nodded and began to think she wouldn't after all enjoy the finale.

"You get tied to that - firmly, mind! No way you're going to escape! And each and every one of us gets to give you a few whacks. Now, some of the girls might go easy but I can assure you the men won't."

She went cold from head to foot, her stomach churned more than it had ever done, even when she confronted the Des lookalike in his dark and sombre inn loaded with spirits and memories, even when she knew the belt would be lashed across her (say it! willing) bottom. Colder than that, for this was many men, and women, who might or might not be kind.

Damien held her arm tightly, not as hard as he had before but hard enough.

"And I'll go last," he told her, which only added to her feeling of awful apprehension.

"Here!" he called to the others, who were emerging from the house, some in couples, others alone. Huge smiles broke out everywhere when they realised it was Abigail who was providing the final rite this time. Marilyn actually shouted:

"Thank goodness it isn't me this time!" which brought laughter from everyone else.

Ralph had the ropes, thick, wiry-looking ropes that would be sure to be rough on her skin. Damien led the silent quaking Abigail to the old tree and untied her wrists.

"Strip!" The arrogance of the command struck deep and with no conscious thought her hands began to pull at her top, then her bra and then she was pulling her shorts down and stepping out of them. She kicked her plimsolls away and tugged her soaking knickers down to stand naked in front of everyone. She resisted the urge to try and use her arms to shield herself from the predatory eyes.

She liked them.

They were sizing her up.

How much could she take?

She was willing to bet no one there had ever felt a birch switch. Her heart swelled with pride and she put her shoulders back, thrusting out her breasts for the greedy eyes of the men.

Somewhere from out of the dusk came a low whistle of admiration, Ralph stepped forwards pulled her towards the tree, immediately stretching her arms around the trunk, pulling her hard against its rough bark. Her nostrils were full of its dusty insecty being. She cradled it, whispered 'help me' as the tree leaned branches down over her, the leaves whispering 'We'll take this, we can' to her frightened ears. Her breasts scraped against the ancient bark and her nipples erected almost instantly. Anticipation began to contend with the fear. Pleasure partnered pride. Nothing could test her as much as Josiah's birching.

Could it?

Ralph wound rope around her waist, wrapped it around her arms, finishing with a large knot the other side of the tree, well out of reach of her fingers. Abigail shuffled her feet, realised she was standing in two depressions, obviously caused by many feet at the end of many games - they fitted too well to be anything but man-made.

"All yours, ladies and gentlemen. Your reward for playing the game this afternoon."

Silence, apart from the rapid breathing and call of late night birds. Abigail imagined she must be silver white in the growing darkness, flushed with red from Ralph's spanking earlier, still dripping from the sex she'd had.

A mixture of emotions, all conflicting: fear of what was to come, excitement at what was to come, passion at the thought of more pain and pleasure.

Marilyn grunted.

"All right, if none of you are going to move." She came close, and Abigail smelled the expensive perfume and cosmetics, felt the pampered, white, soft hand swing against her bottom a couple of times, stinging but leaving no lasting impression.

"That'll do." Marilyn walked off, soft-footed on the grass.

Janet giggled; Abigail recognised the sound. "Now me." She, too, smacked a couple of times, not hard enough to do any real damage. Joy and then Patsy followed. Patsy smacked six times, making her sting a bit.

"Okay, girls, see you later. Thanks for coming." Ralph, dismissing his guests.

"Sure, enjoy yourselves," Marilyn's husky voice again.

Gareth stood by her side, ran a finger down her face, making her shiver. He moved away. "Let's see how it feels." He brought his hand down hard against her cheek, making her yelp. He did it again and again. Stinging, hurting, just with his hand. The tree held her firm let her rub herself against its roughness, took no notice of her face pressed hard against its solid bulk. Only the leaves whispered 'hold on hold on' as Gareth spanked her, hard and firm, bringing a deeper flush, no doubt.

"Over to you, guys."

"It's me." Another face approached, indistinct in the darkness. Barry. "I never found you, much to my disgust. But you'll like this." A thin biting pain shot across her burning cheeks. It reminded her of Mr Lloyd's cane but was a thinner pain; a stupid expression, she told herself, but it's true.

"Cut it especially for you." He brought the switch

down a dozen times, a pause before each one, and each one made her cry out and push against the tree for comfort.

A moment of ease, a moment to feel each thin line burning and hurting, then another voice.

"Can I try that?" There was a moment of rustling and then the switch was handed over.

"Martin here. I didn't find you either, not that I'm complaining, I had enough to do! But Barry made it easy for me, cutting this."

Half a dozen further sharp biting strokes, low down, almost on the thighs, every one bringing a cry from her. She could feel Martin's breath, hot and eager, on the back of her neck. She turned her head, pressed her other cheek against rough bark, dripped a few tears into the crevices. Not able to fight, not able to move, a giving up of all responsibility for what happened. A wave of happiness swept her as she realised she really did like it, despite the pain. It was good, not having any say in it at all. Josiah liked bondage, he tied her wrists the first time.

The ropes held her firm, but not firm enough, her knees could not, would not be allowed to give way.

"John?" Damien making his offer. As if he was her owner. Abigail felt herself getting mad, tugged at the ropes, but they wouldn't move.

"Personally, I prefer a slipper." A stinging slap followed on one cheek. "Making no impression at all after what you did." He aimed the slipper at her thighs, spanking them painfully red. This was not an erotic pain, but a punishment, it really hurt, nerve ends shocked and screamed. Tears crept from her eyes, ran down the trunk, as she moaned 'No, oh oh no," over and over.

Then he stopped, said "Thanks," and walked away, feet crunching on the gravel. Hands rubbed her sore

183

cheeks.

"I had my turn earlier. I'm leaving you to Damien's tender mercies." That was Ralph. Another series of crunching gravel sounds.

And then there was silence, other than the night calls and distant sounds.

Finally there was a rustle of clothes and a movement close by. The air shifted and eddied around her.

"You've been one hell of a girl this afternoon, Abigail, whoever you are, wherever you came from. It's been a long time since anyone took the final game like this. Normally the girls have been screaming and crying and begging to be free and we'd all have to go easy or the other girls would start on us! But you, you're different!" A finger ran down the cleft of her cheeks, found her sensitive places, thrilling her despite the pain. Her bottom ached from its attention, each individual line of the switch left a weal which burned separately from the others.

"You're really different, not once have you asked for mercy. Not once. So I'm going to make you beg."

A whisper of leather. Damien walked around the side of the tree, showed her an instrument of leather thongs, wide, and pliable, attached to a firm handle. Before she could react, before true fear could get hold, he moved away and brought it down across her back. Abigail shrieked as the thongs bit and reddened her soft white skin. She began to cry as the thongs found her again, and then again, across her back, her thighs and her very sore bottom. She pressed her forehead into the bark, hurting herself, feeling every part of her longing to be free, yet ... a part of her was not ready to quit, not yet. Damien lashed her again and her screams lit the dark sky, sending crows cawing into the moonlight, protesting. He did it again and she screamed again. Pain unbelievable, pain everywhere, pain he wanted to give and she wanted to take. It took a dozen lashes before she shouted:

"Stop! Please, please stop! Enough!"

Immediately Damien stopped, put an arm around her shoulders as she sobbed, untied her bonds and took her into his arms.

"God, you're something else!" he murmured into her curls as she cried on his shoulder, rubbing at her bottom with one hand, mopping tears with the other. "Come on, back to the house. I'll find you a stiff drink. I think you'll need it."

She clambered awkwardly back into her clothes.

He led her across the lawn, their turn to crunch gravel, through the porch and panelled hall, where soft light glowed and sombre ancestors stared down at this disreputable and shabby wreck standing in front of them. They went into a small drawing room.

The mirror hung over the hearth.

"I'll get you a drink." Damien pushed her towards a chair. "Wait there. What would you like?"

"Can you find me a rum and lime?" She sniffed and tried to smile. "And I'll just slip upstairs to Janet's room and get my clothes."

"Oh sure, fine, you do that. I won't be long."

Abigail walked stiffly up the long, long flight of stairs, along the corridor, the windows now mirrors of her dishevelled state. The window seats looked comforting and inviting, but she knew she wouldn't be able to sit, walking hurt, moving the sore flesh as she went. More than anything she longed to have a long hot bath, to ease her bruises, to wash away the sex, to take away the dust and grime of rolling in the summer-house, stables and woods. And being crushed against an insect infested dusty old tree, too.

From somewhere along the corridor came the sound of girls chattering and laughing together. Abigail formed some excuses, but Janet's room was empty, in semi-darkness, with only a small lamp lit over the mantel. Abigail slipped out of the borrowed clothes, pulled on the prim dress and wedge heeled shoes and hurried back down the stairs as fast as she could. To hell with the curls, they'd have to stay all over the place.

She was just in time. Damien was coming along the hall, carrying a tray with drinks on it. Before he got into the drawing room she had to get there, and look in the mirror -

"Alfred, could I borrow the red-and-black dress from 'For Glory and For Love?' I've been invited to a fancy-dress ball."

"Sure, Abby, go ahead. We won't be needing it again for some considerable time, I shouldn't think! As I remember, you looked pretty good in it!"

"Yes, but Stevie looked better." Said with a quick smile to Stevie, sitting with Charles in the front row of the auditorium. "Er, Alfred, I'm not sure I'll be able to take part in this play, actually."

"I had you down for a major part, Abby!" Alfred protested but she detected half-heartedness in the words.

She shook her head. "I've got some new projects on the go and they will be somewhat time-consuming." To put it mildly.

"Well, if you're sure..."

"Yes."

Later, as rain softly drifted down from the darkness, turning street lights into glittering displays of fireflies, Abby wandered the streets of Walchurch, carrying the dress wrapped in thick plastic, saying goodbye in the only way she knew.

Some of you will be there in my new life, she thought, ancestors of yours will be there, trading and living their lives as you are now, only in a different time frame. She wandered past the church where she lay sleeping the just sleep of the dead alongside her husband, walked past the noisy rowdy leisure centre where teenagers roller-skated to loud throbbing music. From windows came drifts of television, of radio, raised voices.

Suddenly, very suddenly, Abby despaired of it all. The noises grated on her ears, the music sounded tuneless, the people walking by badly dressed and unfashionable.

With a desperate longing for simpler things, she turned and headed back to her packed and empty flat.

It was time to go. She was tired of the 20th century with all its glitter and commercialism, with its emphasis on consumer goods and not on the quality of life. She had a longing, an overwhelming, almost heart-stopping longing to be walking on rushes on a flagstoned floor, hearing a delicate air played by musicians, hearing the rustle of skirts and the crackle of a huge log fire, hearing Josiah Danverson's solidly strong voice telling her what to do.

It really was time to go.

CHAPTER 34: THEN

Laughter and talk, stiff skirts sweeping the rush-covered floor, jewels sparkling in the light from the fire and the flaming sconces set high on walls. Light also glanced from lace collars; fans fluttered and created their own flares of colour. Small pointed beards, small moustaches, long flowing hair; so elegant these men, so naturally graceful in ribbons and silks. So unlike the men Abigail was used to.

An air of expectation hung over everything, keen glances turning toward the far door where someone was going to make an entrance.

Abigail moved carefully along the stone wall, her naked thighs whispering under her skirts, quim aching with desire - would this be the night she would find the nerve to approach him? She caught sight of herself in a polished shield, glad to see her black hair was dressed just as the ladies had done theirs, with combs and curls, and that the floury mask she had applied fitted well with the look most lades wore. The shield distorted the shape of her face; she knew it was oval, but in her reflection it was more elongated. People looked because she was a stranger, not because she looked out of place.

She hoped her lace collar didn't appear too machine-made. It was different from the rich, expensive and beautiful lace they wore. Abigail couldn't afford hand-made lace.

She moved on toward a tall clouded window, apologising with a nod and a smile for disturbing guests. She received more curious looks but people soon turned away again, back to the door.

Waiting.

A fanfare of trumpets shook castle walls, a boy herald in scarlet doublet and leggings, angelic face, dark hair, perhaps ten years old, stepped in front of the fire, and everyone fell silent.

"My Lord Danverson bids you welcome to the Midsummer Ball!" The high-pitched childish voice carried to the minstrels' gallery. On cue, Lord Danverson entered the hall, ermine robe careless around his shoulders, a doublet glistening with jewels sparkling from the rushlights, huge leather boots rustling as he walked. Abigail noted (again) the broad shoulders, strong legs and harsh profile. She also noticed that no woman accompanied him (again).

"Welcome!" His voice filled corners where shadows hung and ghosts lingered. Someone - a trusted man servant? - handed him a tankard of ale, the wood polished and shining like pewter. "Welcome to Castle Danverson. Musicians, play!" A huge roar went up as he waved the tankard high in the air, foam and ale spilling on to dogs which scampered, barking, at his feet, affected by the tangible excitement of the crowd.

Music began to fill the air, competing with voices and roaring laughter.

"And, people, eat!" Another roar, larger and louder than the first, shook dust from the rafters. Abigail brushed smuts from her scarlet dress, smoothed the black overskirt, tugged at the starched collar and pushed the choker into lace. She had an appearance to maintain in the eyes of strangers.

Men fell on the food with hearty appetites. Women hung back, waiting for the men to clear a space for them. Food. It was the one thing she couldn't do. Not here. She turned back to the window; looked out at rolling downland, fields cultivated in small strips of regular appearance and size. Over it all hung the indefinable sadness of twilight, sun giving way to dark, pinkness giving way to the pressure of purple and then black.

Abigail wished the window was open so she could smell the sadness that tinged the land. It stirred her each time she came here.

"I do not remember seeing you before." A wave of perfume washed around her as Abigail turned to see a dark-haired woman smiling, eyes bright with curiosity. She was wearing a dress of blue overlaying a rich petticoat of gold silk; she had a fluttering fan and eyelashes and a coy smile. Abigail wished she had a chance to get her hands on a dress like that. Or a smile like that.

"No, I ... come from ... far away, just for the ball." Weak, even to her ears. "My Lord's reputation has spread some distance away." That was safe, surely.

"Did you see my Lord's prowess with the falcon in the hunt today?"

"I would rather see my Lord's prowess in bed at night!"

Abigail took a chance with boldness, trusting the look in the eyes didn't let her down. They were talking of the same thing, surely.

The woman's laugh was short and harsh.

"Not I! They say he is a cruel man with a taste for hurting women. But I admire a man who hunts and who can control the falcon as well as my Lord does."

"I would take my chances if I could bed him, for all that."

Abigail glanced at her companion, hoping she'd said it right. There seemed no hint of confusion or suspicion. Talking under rather than over the sound of the minstrels in the gallery helped cover some of the defects in her accent.

"Dance!" bellowed Lord Danverson. Abigail's companion smiled, accepted the arm of a tall blond man in a large padded green doublet encrusted with gold, and moved gracefully into the dance.

"You must talk with me again," she murmured as she left.

Abigail leaned against the windowsill and watched. The castle hall was alive with swirling skirts, lace and gold trimmings. Ladies with starched collars framing their faces rested ring-encrusted hands on their partners' arms, creating a kaleidoscope of colour and movement. Sword hilts sparkled with jewels as the owners moved, hands rarely far from their sides, always alert for any sign of trouble. Were men never at ease with themselves? Abigail wondered.

Smoke from the huge fires hung over everything, disturbed by dancers, by sudden loud shouts from groups of men exchanging pleasantries and jokes at others' expense, standing in corners and near the table.

Abigail shivered. Midsummer, yet it was cold; the fires were welcome. Some guests hugged the flames, in danger of scorching by sparks which leapt from logs. Steam rose from food set out along vast tables stood four square to the floor. Rushes were kicked aside as dancers moved apart and together, swung apart and together again in intricate courtship. Over it all hung the mingled scent of wood ash, food, perfume, dust, mould and body odour. Yet it didn't seem unpleasant to her.

Lord Danverson seemed to be everywhere at once, drinking, shouting, dancing with abandon and gusto, a man who lived life to the full. Abigail saw him look at her, saw the appreciative smile, knew scarlet silk suited her well and that her face was the equal of any at the Midsummer Ball that night.

The dance ended. Lord Danverson left his partner and pushed his way past the guests to approach her.

"Might I enquire if you are enjoying the ball?"

"Yes, my Lord."

"I have seen you here before, but I do not know your name or where you have your home."

"My Lord, I have been a guest at your celebrations on other occasions. I live in a village not far from here. You may know it: Walchurch."

"I know it, but I have no knowledge of the families who live there. And your name?"

A great roar of laughter went up behind Lord Danverson. He smiled and edged closer to Abigail, pinning her against cold stone. Musicians began another dance. Someone bumped into Abigail, half apologised as they moved away, spilling ale from a pewter tankard.

"Abigail Brandon, my Lord." She curtsied as elegantly as she could.

"And on whose arm did you come to the ball tonight?" he leaned against the sill, close, almost whispering. Abigail strained to catch the words.

"I came alone, to see my Lord Danverson."

"Wait for me in my room." It was an order, not a request.

"Yes, my Lord." No questions asked. Accepted. Just as she hoped. He walked away, a smile twisting his dark face. Abigail saw a pageboy standing to one side, anxious, ready to move at command. She beckoned to him.

"Madam?"

"Which is my Lord Danverson's room?"

"On the floor above the gallery, four doors along, a room with blue tapestries and a large bed."

"Thank you. Not a word now, why or what I asked."

The pageboy nodded. He had seen his Lord with her and knew not to ask any questions.

Abigail slipped quietly away, ducking invitations to dance with a smile and shake of her head. Her companion in blue and gold half raised a hand, saw Abigail was leaving and turned back to her companion. Relief - for had she seen machine stitching on the dress, she might have asked questions Abigail could not answer. Not here, not now.

She hurried up the stairs, slippers clicking on the worn stone and thighs whispering their secret as moisture began to seep onto the skin, adding to her barely contained excitement. He had noticed her, he wanted her, he had spoken to her and ordered her to his room. This night she could have him for her very own.

The gallery was chill, the sun leaving the sky to creeping hands of darkness. Thick stone walls had hardly time to become warm before night caught them in an icy grip. Feeble rush lamps flickered and flared in draughts which found their way through velvet hangings and tapestries. She thought (again) England in the summer of 1625 was not really warm enough for her liking.

Lord Danverson's room. The bed was indeed large, draped with blue hangings of rich velvet. It held his sent, smoke, ale, tobacco, leather and cotton. Clothes tossed to one side held the smell of the hunt: horses and woods, blood and sweat. A huge chest stood against a wall, carved with a hunting scene. Abigail ran her hands over it, appreciating the workmanship. Back home, such things were only found in museums, or expensive antique shops. The thought occurred to her that she could become an eminent historian with first-hand knowledge of furniture and antiques, but then they'd wonder how she knew.

And there was the mirror in its ornate frame, hanging over the mantelpiece. It had been moved. Last time it was in one of the drawing rooms, framed by tapestries with wild hunting scenes and mythological stories on them. It had been easy to find. Before she could change her mind, she took the heavy iron poker from the hearth and smashed the mirror into a thousand shards which fell, glittering, onto the rug.

She was grateful for the small fire. Crouching down and lifting her heavy petticoats, she daydreamed. He was as handsome as before, strong long jaw, short pointed beard in the fashion of the day. Dark piercing eyes, Roman nose, a strong handsome face. Would he be good, this man of the manor, of the land, of the whole damn county, by the look of him? Would he be hard and long and would he satisfy her? She could but hope. Surely she hadn't made the journey back again for nothing!

And he had remembered her! Abigail's brief appearances at the castle on the earlier Midwinter and Midsummer feasts had been cautious, moving carefully through the guests, not catching anyone's eye, but waiting her chance. This time she decided to be bold, to experience the man for her own self.

He was long in coming. She huddled on a small stool, then sat on the floor, and finally lay down on a large fur rug stretched before the hearth, dozing and starting awake a dozen times before the door scraped open and she heard slippers coming in.

"I thought you might have left with the others." Slurred with drink, but firm enough for all that. Close to, he was as exciting as she had thought earlier, a lust gleaming in his eyes that brought his face alight. Abigail stood and stretched her arms around his neck, pulling him close, feeling dark stubble graze her face. She breathed in musk, the smell of food, sweat, smoke and manliness that was the greatest aphrodisiac of all. If only it could be bottled and sold! His arms went round her, iron bands holding her close. He darted kisses at her throat, her temple, her nose. She leaned back to look at him.

"My Lord said to wait."

"Yes, but the ball went on longer than I thought."

"I would have waited a thousand days for my Lord." she whispered, pressing against him his muscles hard through her layers of petticoats and hoops. The swelling was there. Her body rarely betrayed her - it conquered the men every time. That and her boldness; they could never stand up to that.

Between kisses he protested: "I do not know who you are..."

"But you do. Abigail Brandon, of Walchurch. What more could my Lord ask? Come." She led him to the bed, pulling on óne work-hardened hand, and sat him on the edge of the huge goose-feather mattress. Then she disrobed slowly, watching his eyes, knowing his excitement. Her soft white skin, heavy full breasts with large nipples, and her plucked pussy, something surely no 17th century man had ever seen, were good for all men. His eyes grew wide and a hand reached out to touch her quim, sliding over the silky whiteness, amazed.

"I have never seen such things - not in my furthest journeyings."

"It is for you and you alone," she whispered, drawing closer to him. He reached out again, hands sliding over her full hips, touching her breasts, the nipples coming erect at his touch. She drew in her breath sharply as one hand found her spine, a finger tracing the length, cupping and smoothing and turning to admire her shape from all angles.

Then he stood up, held her close, kissed her deeply, his breath smelling and tasting of ale and strong meat, a smoky musky smell and taste that thrilled almost as much as the look of his hard muscular body. She moved

196

cautiously against him, not wanting to hurry but wanting him to please, please fuck her and soon. Wet now, wet and willing.

Lord Danverson moved suddenly, pushing her down onto the bed and parting her legs, staring at her as he swiftly undressed, tossing his clothes onto another wild heap on the floor. Then he stood erect, strong, gleaming with lust. She held out her arms, almost groaning at the sight of him. She had waited, she had schemed to get back here, and it had been worth every moment for the sight of him alone.

He climbed onto the bed, knelt between her legs, touched with both hands, letting his fingers slide down her thighs, back up around her hips, up to her navel, under her shaved armpits. He raised his eyebrows but said nothing. She stared at him, tongue pressing between her teeth, sometimes licking her lips, finding him for herself, the heavy balls, hairy and firm, the thick handful she held, touched, caressed, then reached for his buttocks as best she could, grabbing his muscled things, catching his hands at times and pressing them to her quim, begging him without words to do it now.

The length and thickness of his member surprised, shocked, thrilled her as it slid home into her warm waiting body. It filled her completely, pressed against every nerve ending she had. He thrust hard, grunting with pleasure, holding both cheeks in his large hands, again and again finding every part of her. She cried out in sheer pleasure, clawing nails down his back. Every atom reacted to the feeling, shaking her to her toes, she all but swooned. He thrust harder and yet harder, pushing her into the mattress of feather and down. She cried out again, climaxing twice in a blinding sweep of feeling which shut out all thought, all consideration and then swept over her again as he finally came shuddering into her.

He raised himself up and looked at Abigail, an unreadable look, stern yet wondering. She tried to bring herself back down from the high. Something was going on here, she had to cope with it, yet she was longing for more.

Try persuasion.

"Did I please my Lord?" Oh do it again, she thought desperately, do it again! Instead he got up, snatched a robe, flung it around his shoulders and paced the floor. He stopped at times to stare at Abigail, his face unreadable in the mix of light from the rapidly diminishing candle he had brought to his room, and the slowly dying fire.

"You pleased me, but there is something wrong, something I dislike."

"My Lord?"

He appeared to come to a decision and turned toward the bedroom door. "It is the boldness, I think. I can deal with that and I will. Page!"

The door sprang open as if by magic and a small boy stood there, blinking sleep from his eyes.

"Sire?"

"Fetch me a birch!"

The boy looked scared but said "Sire!" and the door closed again.

"A ... birch?" stammered Abigail, pushing herself up the bed, getting away from the gleam of pure malice which had replaced the one of lust.

"A birch, my lady, a birch - for the pretty cheeks which were so keen to be dealt with in one way must be dealt with in another." He leaned across the bed and caught hold of her wrists with hands as hard as iron, dragging her toward the bedpost. Then she was on her feet, both hands being held together on one side of the post, shivering with post orgasmic pleasure and a touch of fear. Events were taking a turn she had not anticipated and it was a bit scary. Lord Danverson grinned as he slid the girdle from his robe and bound her wrists tightly with the silken length. Around and around hr wrists, pulling her veins close together, so close she could feel her pulse. Abigail bit her lips, looked at Lord Danverson with pleading eyes, saying 'let me go' without uttering the words.

Suddenly she remembered the woman from the ball:

'Not I, for they say he is a cruel man with a taste for hurting women.'

"I do not know from where you came, or why you are here with me, but those who offer their bodies are wanton hussies and are dealt with in the time-honoured way, madam." The last word was said with sarcasm and malice. The gleam of lust was back again - this man did indeed have a taste for hurting women. Abigail was suddenly very cold. His come trickled down her thigh, cool and sticky and she became aware of a real tinge of fear for the first time since she had started visiting Castle Danverson.

But underneath the fear was the excitement of yet another new experience and she knew that, even if she could see herself in the mirror, she wouldn't. Wouldn't send herself dizzyingly flying forward through hundreds of years. To safety. And of course she couldn't. What if she wanted to change her mind right now, when the moment of truth was close...

Your choice.

But a birch? Fear sat coppery-tasting in her mouth, her body shivering despite the fire. She could not see Lord Danverson but she sensed him standing very still, very tense, very exited, and wondered again what was to happen. One thing was sure: she could not twist this man around her finger as she had the others, oh so many others.

It seemed an age before the door opened again and the small boy's voice said: "The birch, sire."

The door closed. Lord Danverson had not spoken. Abigail stared at the rich hangings of the four poster bed, stared at the carved headboard with its cornucopia of fruit and birds, felt rather than saw him walk around her, eyeing her carefully.

"Now, madam, we will deal with wanton hussies who offer themselves to their Lord." A thousand bees stung her at once as the birch connected with her bare bottom. She cried out, gasping in pain and shock as it landed, again and again.

"On my territory, women are taught to obey their men in all things and that, madam, includes the question of who he is to take to his bed." The many strands found her, tiny buds causing their own pain, sharp wet twigs flexible enough to bend on impact, to send fire through her. She fought the pain and the bonds, but he went on birching her, forcing her into the post, her pubis grinding against the carving as she tried to squirm away from the stinging biting burning sensation. Tears coursed down her face, tears of helplessness as much as cursing herself for her stupidity. Never get out of sight of the mirror! she told herself, crying out as the birch found her again.

"My sentence is always the same for those who commit misdemeanours here, madam." A pause in the agony, just his relentless voice lecturing her on the wilful nature of her crime. Lord Danverson was not a man to be crossed at any time!

Oh let that be it! she pleaded and prayed silently, waiting, quivering, hurting, as he walked backwards and forwards, slippers hushing on the wooden floor. Somehow she knew it would be a waste of breath to plead aloud for mercy and clemency.

"My sentences for wayward hussies, women who should know better, is 50 strokes of the birch. Madam, you have had 25. There are 25 to go."

She was hurting so much, surely he had drawn blood! No one could hurt this much and not bleed!

"Stand and wait."

She had no choice, hands bound round the post as they were. Tears continued to pour down her face, she longed to wipe them away.

"Sire..."

"Be silent! It is not done for a woman to entice a man in such a way - no respectable woman! You came with no man, I asked them all! You belong to no one! Did you come with the intention of finding my room? Be warned, wench, I do not usually consort with wanton women but it is midsummer and you intrigued me. Now you will pay the price of that intrigue, whoever you are."

Abigail bit her lips, afraid of spilling the truth. Not that Lord Danverson would believe she had come from hundreds of years in the future, anyway.

He began to birch her again, this time finding her thighs and legs. The pain was intense and gave her superhuman strength. Even as she cried out her despair and fear, the girdle gave way and she was free. She looked at Lord Danverson, and fell at his feet.

"Sire, forgive me, I had to find a way to be with you!"

Was he listening? The birch was dropped to the bedroom floor and he stared at her, open-mouthed in shock.

"If I did not know better, I would have said you enjoyed that, wench."

She looked up at him, all her love and devotion shining clear in her eyes.

"Oh yes, I would take that and more from my Lord

Danverson."

He moved over to her, raised her up with strong hands under her armpits, held her close, buried his hands and then his face in her mass of black curls, then kissed her deeply. She melted under his lips and elegant curled beard.

"This is not a dream," he murmured.

"No dream, my Lord, but reality. I have come and if you wish it, sire, I shall stay."

"Oh yes, you shall stay. I have long wanted ... "

His hands found her burning cheeks, held and squeezed them, and then he slapped her, hard. She cried out, muffled against his chest, but did not attempt to pull away.

"Take me again," she whispered. He scooped her up in his arms and laid her back on the goose-feather mattress. No foreplay this time, just her open arms and his cock as hard and as thick and as strong as before. He slid into her, riding the residue of his own juices and hers, mingled irrevocably and eternally in her waiting willing body. He crushed her into the mattress, filled every part of her body and her mind.

Abigail mused.

"In the morning I'll burn the dress - when he finds me something else to wear - and find me a wise woman to curse the site of our castle, so nothing is ever built but a castle or a theatre. And sweep up the pieces of mirror which, miracle of miracles, he hasn't noticed."

Over her Lord's shoulder Abigail glanced at the mirror and saw with shock it hung unbroken in its frame, reflecting the room, not the future. It had become a normal mirror, fit for looking in. She smiled with pure happiness.

"What amuses you, my lady?" he traced a finger down her face, looking deep into her eyes, wondering, yet assured.

"Nothing, my Lord. Only the pleasure of being in your bed and at your service in any way you please."

To hell with the twentieth century, she thought, tensing her muscles against the man so full within her. She was too busy here.

Too busy being a slave in time.

COINS

BY JOSEPHINE SCOTT

Coins. Two of them: shiny, bright, new, clinking together in my hand. Not in my purse, no: here in my hand, gloved against the cold.

Why do gravestones look so stark in winter and yet so benign in summer? Does the sun really change the stone that much?

Could the sun have changed and warmed you, I wonder?

But if it had, you would not have been the Master I met.

The source of all my fantasies and rush of adrenaline – even now, as I stand before your grave and read the words.

One year gone.

One long year of mourning and sadness, of grief and bereavement I could not and cannot and will not share with anyone.

Not even the master I have now.

Oh the memories! All brought back by standing here, coins in my hand. Here, let me sit: bench cold under my legs, touching the backs of my knees, that oh-so-tender place you touched so gently with the riding crop before bringing it down across the back of my thighs, scaring me half to death that you would strike my legs - I cannot bear my legs to be whipped. You threatened, you teased and tormented with that touch. First the fear of being whipped there, then the pain of feeling it across my thighs, mixed with the relief it didn't strike my legs – a strange heady mixture, adrenaline rushing everywhere at once, explosive and wild and wonderful.

A touch as light as the coins I now hold in my hand.

The cemetery is empty.

No, that's not true and you would punish me with whip and crop, with cane and tawse, with loud words and pain that –

Coins.

The cemetery is not empty, it is full; mouldering bodies and bones at rest, memories which live on beneath the earth, stored away. Dig beneath the stones here and a treasure house of memories, of stories, of longing, regrets and fantasies fulfilled will come rushing out, thick as locusts, to cling to the branches of the great chestnut tree which weeps its empty tears into the depths of sorrow that so many 'In Loving Memory' inscriptions tell to the world.

How true are they?

Is it true that perjury is committed every time a gravestone is carved?

Not always. The biggest devil has a streak of angel in them somewhere, even if it is smothered by years of development, of aching anger and hatred of penury and poverty, of amassed wealth and power –

How you would laugh at me were I to say these things out loud! Were you able to sit there, atop the gravestone, your legs crossed in that contrary, elegant and yet provocative way you had. What would you say to me now?

Demand I kneel at your feet, to do homage to a Master, feel the touch of a hand, the caress of the cane, before it whipped down so hard – and so many times – while I waited, patiently waited, for your bidding to let me up again?

It wasn't like that, was it?

Not at first.

There was so much to learn and I thought I had gone through the learning process with my Master, chosen by answering advertisements with care, chosen by studying the words not written on the page, picking the man who offered to be Master, not one who demanded, for in a new relationship there must be trust, and how much trust must there be in a Master/slave relationship when you are new and scared and lonely and afraid of what you are?

I was afraid.

I never told you this, not ever, not when we were in darkness and you demanded my secrets. Never told you how afraid I was when choosing a Master.

Imagine. A young woman, lonely and experiencing feelings she should never have felt, not without a man around. Turned on by stories of spanking, court cases, stories snatched here and there, illicit-bought books from Private Shops, drooled over in the comfort of a bed made warm with heat of wanting and desire.

Buying the magazines, seeing the advertisements, each an opening plea for someone, anyone, to visit Masters so they too could use up the burning heat they experience at nights, when beds are lonely and slaves few. Loneliness is the biggest problem; being lonely because you are afraid to get into a relationship, afraid of asking a man, afraid of what they will think, what they will do.

Say you want and they think you're a slut.

Don't say what you want and go lonely and aching to bed, unsatisfied.

Answer an advertisement. So many, all differently worded, all saying the same thing; come to me come to me come to me...

Study the replies. What do they say, what do they not say, will they agree to talk, to write, to learn to trust before the moment of meeting comes? Ignore those who issue demands from the start – no way are they the men you are seeking, I am seeking, no way any woman taking those first tentative steps would respond to a man like that. There is no way a man like that is a true Master.

Answering the ones who talk of limits and abiding by them; perhaps hoping they will go over the limits, to take you into the realms of pure ecstasy that a non-submissive cannot and never will be able to understand.

He was kind, my Master. He was good to me. We talked on the phone, we discussed by letter, pages and pages of fantasies and longings and shared experiences; loneliness of not being able to get what we wanted, how we hoped the coming together would work and if it worked, what fun we could have.

And we met, my Master and I, and we talked in neutral territory, a comfortable pub with an open fire, red leather seats, wooden tables showing deep richness put there by beer, polish and bodies. We met and we talked over drinks, clink of glass, reminding me now of the clink of coins.

Oh, he was kind, my new Master. We went back to his flat, exclusive, expensive and luxurious; there I found I could undress, reveal breasts that ached for the touch of the strap and pussy that ached for the touch of the martinet and cheeks which ached for everything that was going, not that he gave it me all at once, you understand, no way. He took it steady, slowly, a spanking, a light one but it left me hot and wriggling and …

Yes, admit it, longing for more. And more I got by going back later, by going back at another time and taking more, moving from hand to slipper to strap.

When he thought I was ready and could learn to kneel at his command, to be silent when told, to wear a collar and look proud when doing it, he moved on, taught me to know my place, to be obedient to his every wish.

And moved on again, to the deep hurting pain of the

tawse which I took on body and cheeks, on legs and hands, at his wish and thrilled to the obeying of his commands. Thrilled as much for the obeying as to the pain and the afterglow, which is second to none and there is no none when there is a Master like this,

He moved me on. In six months I was fully trained, able to take the whip, the cane, the tawse, the martinet, whatever he wished I could take and did.

And rejoiced in the taking.

Then it all changed.

And how!

My orders were simple and direct. An address, a time, a place. Once a month for six months,

To visit you.

Regardless of what he did to me in the meantime, regardless of what bruises, weals and feelings I brought with me, I had to come to you.

I never knew when or how you worked this out between you, I did not dare ask!

The first time, remember the first time? Shy, nervous, shaking inside and you so cold, so hard, so determined. We talked – no, I lie, you talked of your wishes, how I would learn to take what you gave without movement, without flinching, without a sound. I went the first time bruiseless, if there is such a word, such a state but later I went bruised and sore, to make your punishments harder to take. Bruised outside and inside, still learning to devote myself to my Master, still learning not to be proud in his presence but to keep my eyes to the ground, my voice to a whisper, my demeanour demure as long as I wore his collar.

With you it was different.

You had no use for a collar.

You had coins.

Undressed, surveyed and cold cold coins placed on

my shoulders: lose them and I faced a repeat of what I had when I lost them.

I lost them.

Time and time again, the coins slipped and fell, soundless, to the carpet. I would see their silver eyes wink at me and knew I had to endure the tawsing, the caning, the crop, the whip, whatever it was your pleasure and your delight to use on me, over again.

And each time the coins fell.

And after the coins and the implements had fallen, the darkness, single candle flame, flickering, mesmerising candle flame before my eyes and you asked questions and I told secrets and you made me be logical in my answers.

I was good by the fourth month and by the sixth month no coins fell. Not once.

With a huge sigh you told me my training was done and I could return to my Master, knowing I would never have to come again.

If I had known about the imminent heart attack – but then I am not psychic, it is enough to know I had given you pleasure at the end of your life and that, my dear friend, is more than many women can say.

So here I am. A cold winter's morning. The only living person in a cemetery of aching bones and stored memories. What memories you have in your head I cannot say. My secrets are there and I have come today to share the last one, my fear and terror of finding, and of not finding, a man.

Well, you know I have one. My Master is delighted with me, with my performance as a slave and as a woman.

Most of it is thanks to you.

Here I am with coins in my hand, my final gift to a man who gave me so much pleasure, albeit later, when the pain went and the memories began. I wanted to say thank you for the memories. I don't know who chose your gravestone, but it is just right. It has that high curve in the centre, sweeping down to the two shoulders.

It is there I place my coins.

FROM MY WINDOW

BY JOSEPHINE SCOTT

Secrets.

We all have them. It's just that some have more than others.

Look. Easy goes the man in white overalls. He's our local painter and decorator, drives a little van with his name on the side, both sides actually, and he is an oft-seen figure working around town. No one takes any notice.

So I ask myself, as I see him from my window, why he treks so slow and easy along the footpath to the house in the next road, who are obviously not having painting and decorating done? (How do I know? No paint goes in.)

What did go in were the ladders. I imagine, in the deep recesses of my mind, the ladder leaning against the wall. I imagine the lady of the house stripped-as-she-was-born naked under the command of her Master, he of the white overalls and paint-splashed hands. Naked and quivering a little, nipples erect, quim oozing, in anticipation of-

He orders her forward, she leans against the cool aluminium rungs, reaches her hands above her head as he insists she grips those cold, cold rungs. Chilled now, she gasps as the rungs bite into belly and thigh, into collar bones as the melon-heavy tits hang through the space where feet should go.

Feet guided to each side of the ladder as it leans. Now she is displayed, as coldly displayed as any lobster on a cold, cold slab. Lobsters are blue and black when they are cold, red when they are hot. She will be red when he is through.

There are no preliminaries, they both know why he has come. The large brush which is used for pasting wallpaper is also good as a paddle and he applies it, hard, to both cheeks, bang bang bang until she is pink and gasping and tugging at the bonds. The wooden handle and stem, the binding of metal and bunching of fibre hairs all combine to become an effective discipline instrument. No words, just smacks, hard, steady, no chance to breathe in between stroke, she is wriggling and quivering and begging.

He stops.

The brush is trailed from thigh through crack to back, the hairs tickling and touching, exciting and awakening. She stands, helpless, while he goes to the front of her, where the ladder is angled against the wall and her face is inches from his, her tits even fewer inches.

Another brush, a two inch special, finest hairs, brushed backwards and forwards across erect quivering sensitive nipples, encouraging them to greater swollen throbbing sensitivity. Waves of orgasm shatter through her, this lady with melon breasts and rounded stomach, whose bush is invitingly thick and thighs invitingly round. The two inch brush finds a new home.

Back to the back. The red cheeks are now turning pink, the pain of the spanking easing back. Slowly he reaches inside his white overalls, so large they can hide anything, even a huge throbbing erection and draws out, with a whisper of leather on cloth, a belt. She tenses, knowing what is to come, knowing this will be the climax. The two inch brush is clenched tight in weeping quim.

The belt lashes out, cracks with authority across cheeks exposed and waiting; sheer authority alone out there in the first place.

Belt cracks again and again, up to twelve times, twelve authoritative cracks of a leather strap disguised as a belt by the addition of buckle and holes, but which we all know is an instrument of discipline which men wear as a sign of dominance over women.

Each crack a shriek, each stripe of pain a reason to press against the rung and clutch tight on the slippery varnished handle of the two inch brush.

And then the two inch brush is removed and a seven inch cock is put in its place, from within the capacious white overalls.

And the man with the white overalls strolls home along the footpath, whistling as he goes, hands in pockets, and I see him from my window.

And I wonder.

From my window I see the man next door go out, tight butt in tight shorts, racquet in bag and gold chain around the neck. He is so much a ladies' man, so much the sort who will wink at any female under twenty-one. I know, I have seen him, from my window.

I cannot see him once the car turns round at the top of the road and disappears. But in imagination I can go anywhere and I do.

A leisure club for sure, a fitness and health gym, certainly. And – I go.

The club is full of sweating athletic bodies. The sauna is full of naked sweating athletic bodies who are not ashamed to drop a towel and reveal all.

And in the main work-out areas, bodies. Bodies doing press-ups, doing Step when everything moves as you leap the Step and down again, rhythmic stamping of feet, rhythmic swinging of arms, triceps curl, biceps swing. Tense those muscles, squeeze that butt, curl that stomach, strengthen those legs.

Wrap them around my waist when you're through?

My Man Next Door has played a vigorous game of

tennis. He has cracked that racquet from one end of the court to the other, has smashed the ball against the ground, the net, the partner's racquet, has dripped and sweated and felt himself rubbing against those tight tight shorts, felt both cheeks juddering under the impact, the shock of movement up the legs and into the thigh muscles translated into hanging balls of pure lust.

And his partner is blonde, sharp and exciting, who has sweated and dropped as much as he has, but whether her quim has rubbed at her shorts is anyone's guess.

But fresh from the game, they are both ready for shower and for a session of lust.

Oh, let's call it what it is, for he will go home to his wife and she to her husband, so why not call it what it is?

Delicate. A finger touching on a steaming pussy, touching the love bud, touching the lips which scream at the touch. And in turn she touches the joyously crying head as the thick blue vein pulses in the side and the blood flows strong and the cock stiffens and it slides oh how it slides as she is slammed against the wall as the ball slammed against the net. And she has nowhere to go so the hands slide round, the body tips over and he has her across the bench in the shower room, wet steaming bench, wet steaming towels, wet steaming body. And a hand, pink from the shower, hard from the racquet, which descends over and over again while she squeals and wriggles and gasps and pleads for mercy and he knows this game is one he has won. It is her penalty for winning.

And they shower again, fast, to rid themselves of the evidence and he goes home with a smile and a look and a wave and a call. "All right?" which is all I see and hear from my window.

And I wonder.

I turn from my window where I have watched my family depart for a shopping trip. I turn away and look at the secret drawer which contains my secret, the vibrators and the creams. And I slide open the drawer, slide out the long thin white vibrator with its finely pulsing head and the three inch vibrator with its buzzing angry body and the thick vibrator made to look like the real thing, eight inches long and thick, thick around and with two speeds. Today it will be fast.

And the small vibrator slides in the back and the big vibrator slides in the front and the long thin one is used to tease the love bud and I stand at the wardrobe and select for myself, this time, a tawse which can be sent around the back, to whip across cheeks so lightly yet stinging, to bring back the memory of the time it landed twenty stinging times and I pleaded but got them all.

No one looks in my window.

No one knows my secret sessions.

I can stand at my window and look down at you, a vibrator in every orifice, trembling and shuddering as the feelings overtake me.

And you will never, never, know.

Trojan Slaves
Syra Bond

The army of the Greeks is encamped outside the walls
of Troy and the legendary war rages all around. So when
Sappho and Chrysies, two beautiful Trojan girls are
captured by their deadly enemies trying to flee the city,
their situation is not a good one.

The question of who will possess and dominate the
two slaves becomes the source of friction within the
Greek camp and the two hapless captives can only pray
that some miracle will help them escape from the cruel
and warlike men into whose hands they have fallen.

Silver Moon

Trojan Whores

Syra Bond

As the great Trojan war moves towards its catastrophic end, the beautiful Trojan captives Sappho and Chryseis struggle to survive in the hostile camp of the Greeks. They are the helpless playthings of powerful men who fight each other for the spoils of war.

Praxis and Ajax, Achilles and Polydorus, slave traders and warriors alike want their share of the plunder from the ruins of Troy. The two girls are simply desirable flotsam
to be exploited and used by whoever possesses them.

Trojan Whores provides more non-stop erotic action from the pen of Syra Bond.

Africanus is a beautiful North African girl enslaved by Rome from an early age and then given a chance to train at a 'ludus' for a career as a gladiatrix. Her owner's business affairs depend on her success in the arena but immediately she becomes the centre of a web of deceit.

The treacherous slave girl Nydia spies on her. The lady Octavia, wife of her owner is having a torrid affair with the games sponsor and the creditors are closing in on the ludus.

Filled with all the decadence, sex and danger of life in ancient Rome, the first instalment of Africanus' adventures is a headily erotic read in the best traditions of Silver Moon books.

Africanus, the beautiful black slavegirl has escaped the brutality of the arenas in Imperial Rome but her ship is wrecked far to the north and she finds herself a prisoner of the Celts.

The warriors lose no time in taking full advantage of such an unexpected piece of good fortune and for Africanus it seems as though her fate is sealed.

However, worse awaits her as she finds herself swept up in savage rituals from which she barely escapes with her life. To make matters even worse she earns the enmity of the Celts' High Priestess herself.

From the brothels of the legions' garrison towns and their arenas, to the sinister standing stones in the forests, Ritual of Pain features an intensely erotic array of beautiful slavegirls, and dominant masters and mistresses who are all intent on possessing Africanus' body.

In this volume you will find some of the very best of
the best! Silver Moon's top authors give you a glimpse
into parts of their characters' worlds that we haven't
seen yet. In a series of brilliant 'spin-off' stories, they
widen the pleasure of those readers who already know
their work and give new readers a dazzling insight into
the erotic heart of the Silver Moon catalogue.

Sweet Submissions Volume 2

Kim Knight's Mia is left at the scene of a minor car crash by the driver. A police car arrives but her troubles are very far from being over.

A woman awakes to find herself in the hands of a satanic cult in Richard Garwood's tale.

Syra Bond's story of a strange meeting on a hot night in New Orleans is hauntingly erotic.

Sean O'Kane's story, simply entitled 'Slave' will stay in the reader's mind for a long time.

Caroline Swift contributes a 'lost' incident from her novel 'The Sufferers'.

Falconer Bridges gives us a teasing glimpse into his forthcoming novel.

William Avon contributes a characteristically sharp account of a woman in captivity.

Silver Moon's authors dish up another feast of piquantly erotic fiction such as only they can devise!

Painful Performances

Silver Moon

Richard Garwood

Curiosity may have killed the cat but for Sarah it leads to a life changing experience. When she decides to try on a piece of fetish clothing her boyfriend brings home for a photo shoot, her punishment launches them both onto a bizarre career path.

Performing for ever more demanding audiences, Sarah sinks deeper and deeper into the role of submissive. But once she is taken away to train for a mysterious club and from then on there is no turning back...

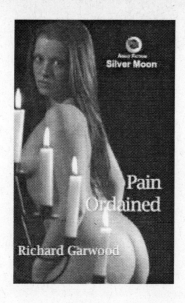

In 'Pain Ordained' Richard Garwood creates visions of powerfully erotic submission and domination. Some are unusual and surprising, some are dark and thrilling, but all are highly charged reading for those who relish excursions into the farther reaches of sexuality.

There are over 100 stunningly erotic novels of domination and submission in the Silver Moon catalogue. You can see the full range, including Club and Illustrated editions by writing to:

Silver Moon Reader Services
Shadowline Publishing Ltd,
No 2 Granary House
Ropery Road,
Gainsborough,
Lincs. DH21 2NS

You will receive a copy of the latest issue of the Readers' Club magazine, with articles, features, reviews, adverts and news plus a full list of our publications and an order form.